Anna and the Missing Child

Anna and the Missing Child

Quentin Academy of Magical Arts and Sciences

Brigitte Novalis

Novalis Press

Published by Novalis Press

ISBN 978-1-944870-32-4

Typesetting services by BOOKOW.COM

Acknowledgments

I thank you,
Susanne Hoeppner
and Torsten Zimmer,
for your valuable artistic
and linguistic advice!

Chapter 1

Departure

When Anna woke up, she immediately remembered that the feared first day of September had come, the day she was to fly to the Quentin Academy of Magical Arts and Sciences.

She was now ten years old, and it was time for her to go to school, whether she wanted to or not.

And she did not want to.

It didn't matter how excited her parents were or what they had told her about the interesting things she would learn there. The thought of going left her cold. She could also do without the new friends she would meet there. The only ray of hope was that her friend Julius, who had also turned ten, would go to school there too. But her life was perfect just as it was.

Why couldn't things stay the way they were? Why did everything have to change?

The Quentin Academy was not far from home. Her parents had studied there, as had her uncles, aunts, and grandparents. All of them. And they had seemed to like it.

But she wanted to stay at home. She wanted to help Martha with her plants and Henry in his workshop. And Bennie desperately needed his big sister. Here everything was familiar and beautiful. Where in the world could it be better?

"Good morning," said the frog beside her pillow. "Time to get up."

Well, it was not a real frog, just a magical toy frog that woke her up in the morning at the time she'd told it to the night before.

"Oh, give me five more minutes," she said. "It's just so cosy in bed."

The frog rolled his eyes

She closed her eyes, snuggled into the soft pillows of her bed, and listened to the birds. Whole flocks of birds chirped, whistled, and tweeted in her garden. She could have listened for hours.

“Last chance to get up,” said the frog after five minutes.

“Yes, yes, relax.”

She took off her nightshirt and went to the sanitary chamber and then to her fresh chamber. Which of her favourite scents did she want? Lavender, pine, or chamomile? Pine. Yes, pine would help her really wake up. What about the temperature and strength? She chose cool and medium. How refreshing it was to have her body and hair rinsed by an air stream of purifying energies!

When she came back to her room, she petted the magical frog and went to the chest where the clothes the school had sent lay.

Everything was different from what she was used to—the socks and shoes, even the underwear, and most of all the school uniform, which was a cherry-red tunic with cherry-red pants. Sighing, she dressed.

As she walked to the door, she could not help looking into the mirror. Actually, the school uniform looked quite good. But to wear a school uniform for five days every week—what a terrible thought!

When she came into the kitchen, she stopped in the doorway. The morning light shone through the windows, filling the kitchen with its splendor and making the pansies in the window boxes glow. The golden light shone on the kitchen utensils on the counter; on the round table in the middle of the kitchen with the white cups, plates, and bowls on it; and on Martha sitting at the kitchen table drinking coffee.

She saw Martha lay her right hand on the multi-faceted disc-shaped crystal that hung from a gold chain around her neck. Her mother closed her eyes and smiled. In the next moment paintings of flowers appeared on the cups and plates, the same pansies as in the window boxes.

"Good morning," Anna said.

"Good Morning! Oh, Anna, how pretty you look in your school uniform." Martha got up and hugged her. With a soft purr, Martha's black and white cat, Katinka, clung to her legs.

Henry, who was baking pancakes, waved to her and said with a smile, "Good morning, Anna. You always look pretty."

Hector, his golden retriever, greeted her with his tail wagging and a loving gaze in his golden eyes.

"How about coffee this morning?" Martha asked.

She had actually been planning to drink raspberry tea. Nevertheless, she said “yes” because she usually was not allowed to drink coffee.

“Where is Bennie?”

“He’s playing in the garden. Can you get him, please?”

Benjamin did not play in the garden. He also did not respond to her calls. She found him behind the hedge in the meadow. There he sat in the grass and laughed softly.

Some chickens walked in front of him. Only they did not just walk; they paraded in a row. When Anna arrived, the chickens walked from left to right then they stopped briefly, turned around, and walked from right to left.

“Bennie, no, you must not do this,” she said.

Benjamin started to cry.

“Stop it, Bennie! Leave the chickens alone!”

But the chickens continued in one line. Now they walked from left to right again.

“Bennie,” she cried, “stop it!”

Benjamin looked at her, frightened, and the chickens ran, loudly cackling, in all directions.

"Playing with chickens is fun." Benjamin said, sobbing.

"You may have fun, but the chickens only have fun if they can do what they want. You must not force them to do what you want."

Benjamin wept louder.

"Don't cry," she said. "Come on, let's go inside. Dada is baking pancakes."

"With syrup?" Benjamin asked and stopped crying.

"With syrup. I can even drink coffee today."

"I also drink coffee."

"I doubt that."

Hand in hand, they walked into the house through the garden between the flowerbeds filled with fragrant flowers and herbs.

To Anna, the coffee tasted bitter and could only be endured with lots of sugar and milk. The pancakes were as good as ever, but she could hardly eat. Her neck was constricted.

Soon she would have to go to school, away from Henry, Bennie, Hector, and Katinka; away from the flocks of birds in the garden; away from her home, all day long.

"Don't be sad," said Martha. "School is fun, and you come back home every afternoon. You're also here on the weekends."

"Yes, but everything will be different now."

Just as she thought she could not hold back her tears any longer, she heard a whooshing sound outside, some energetic steps, and Norbert's cheerful voice.

"Were you going to eat all these delicious pancakes without me?" he asked as he sat down at the table.

"Norbert!" Benjamin exclaimed enthusiastically.

"We still have some for you," Henry said and put a pancake on a plate for him.

"Good to have you here. May I pour you coffee as usual?" Martha asked.

"Gladly. I need sustenance if I want to help Henry with his today's experiment," Norbert said.

"Thank you for coming to help me. But yesterday I looked at the problem again from different angles, and now I have set up the experiment in such a way that I only have to be there for a few minutes every hour. So, everything is under control. I'm sorry you have come in vain."

"Come in vain? Then I would have missed these delicious pancakes. And most of all, the historic event of Anna flying to the Quentin Academy for the first time! That's today, right?"

"Norbert, would you perhaps come along with us to the Quentin Academy?" Anna asked.

"Would I come along? Are you kidding? With the greatest pleasure," Norbert said before digging into his pancake.

She watched Norbert eat and drink with enthusiasm. Norbert's brown eyes shone, and his brown hair curled more wildly than Henry's hair. Norbert was not only as slim and tall as Henry, his younger brother, but downright long and thin.

"Who else is coming along?" Norbert asked with a full mouth.

He raised his coffee cup to be refilled.

"Me, me!" Benjamin shouted.

"Actually, I wanted to go with Anna," said Martha. "Henry and Bennie stay at home."

"Then I have the pleasure of accompanying two beautiful ladies," said Norbert. "Oh, I wish I had put on my embroidered silk vest for this special occasion!"

Anna laughed, but then they had to go. Henry took her firmly in his arms. How often had she gone to her father when she was hurt or afraid, and how often had he comforted her, helped her, and cheered her up?

"Take it easy, my girl," he said softly.

She nodded.

Benjamin clung to her legs. "I come with you," he said. "I am really good. I come with you."

"Anna will come back this afternoon."

"Anna has to stay here."

"Anna can't stay here, but you can help me in the workshop," Henry said. "Besides, I have a surprise for you."

"A surprise? What kind of surprise? Anna, come with me," Benjamin said, pulling her by the hand.

"Just three minutes?" she asked. Martha nodded.

She followed Benjamin and Henry to the workshop where Henry's magical devices stood at various stages of completion on the tables and shelves. Lights flashed on one of the devices. That had to be the experiment.

"Look here, Bennie. This is for you."

Henry put a white magic toy mouse on the ground, which ran away from Benjamin and hid itself. Fortunately, the mouse ran slowly enough that Benjamin was able to catch it. Her little brother laughed.

When Anna sat down next to Martha and Norbert on the carpet, Hector came up beside her and handed her his paw, which he rarely did. Then Hector stepped back, and Norbert switched on the force field around the carpet, which would protect them on the flight.

"To the Quentin Academy of Magical Arts and Sciences," Norbert said to the carpet, and the carpet immediately took off, flying higher and higher.

The house and garden grew smaller. Meadows and woodlands spread below them. In the distance, Anna could see the Atlantic shining in the sunlight.

"Norbert, Anna's friend Julius lives down there." Martha pointed to a long house under tall maple trees. "I wonder if the Aquilases have already left."

As soon as Martha said this, the carpet went down into a steep dive, curving between the trees and around the Aquilases' house. Anna clung to Martha. A dog barked. A peacock shrieked.

"Behave yourself!" Norbert warned, tapping on the carpet. "Head back toward the Quentin Academy."

The carpet flew up again, turned to the west, and curled up its sides.

Anna could breathe again. She could even speak.

"Why does it do this? I mean curling up its sides?"

"I'm not sure. Maybe that's its laughter."

The carpet flew farther to the west. In the distance, a few houses appeared and then more and more houses, embedded in gardens. Some houses clustered around a grass court. Down below them was the town of Oakville.

On the western edge of Oakville, a long building with two side wings and a park in the back came into view.

“Quentin Academy of Magical Arts and Sciences,” Martha said.

She took Martha’s hand.

Chapter 2

Arrival

As the carpet descended, Anna saw adults in brightly colored dresses and suits, some in black robes, and between them children in cherry-red school uniforms that matched her own, standing and walking in the square in front of the academy.

She thought she recognized Julius with his parents, but before she could be sure, the carpet turned, circled around the academy, and touched down behind the building on a landing site in front of a large open hall.

Martha, Norbert and she got up from their carpet. Norbert pressed his hand on the edge of the carpet and the carpet rolled tight. At its edge appeared the text *Cameron, Norbert*.

"Allow me, dear Martha, to show Anna where the carpets are parked."

Norbert took the carpet under his arm and led them into the hall. Adults in colorful clothes and children in cherry-red school uniforms came towards them, while others were busy at the compartments.

"The carpets of guests are in the left rear corner of the hall."

Norbert headed for it and put his carpet in a compartment. Immediately afterwards a label with the name *Cameron, Norbert* appeared at the bottom of the compartment.

"The compartments on the right rear corner are for teachers and study companions, and all the other compartments are for students. The compartments are arranged alphabetically. Want to find yours?"

"I already have a compartment?" Anna searched along the walls. "Up there, I see something that looks like *Cameron*, but it's too high for me."

Norbert pulled a low silvery platform close, which had a railing on the left, back, and right. It hovered a hand's breadth above the ground.

"Would you stand on this platform for a moment? If you press the red button here, you'll notice how it starts to move and goes up."

She stood on it, put her left hand on the railing and pressed with the right hand on the red button.

"Hey, it's going up." She clung to the railing.

"Keep pressing the button until you are right in front of your compartment."

She found the compartment with the label *Cameron, Anna*, and inside it a carpet that was also labeled with her name.

"I have my own carpet? And I can use it to fly all by myself?"

"Yes, isn't that a nice surprise? The director will explain everything to you afterwards. First, please press the blue button until you are down again. You can also move the platform slightly to the left or to the right when you're on the ground."

Actually, that was fun.

"Now let's first look for our friends. Maybe there's even something to eat and drink here," Norbert said. Martha laughed.

Anna walked between Martha and Norbert around the building to the forecourt, which was teeming with people. There were so many unknown people! If only she could find Julius!

"Norbert!" someone called. "What a surprise! I did not know you were married!"

A black-haired man with a mustache pressed his way through the crowd. Behind him he pulled a girl with dark eyes and a long black braid over the left shoulder of her cherry-red uniform.

With a laugh, the man patted Norbert's shoulder. "I'm glad to see you again after so many years! Would you introduce me to your wife and daughter?"

"Martha, allow me to introduce you to my friend Gabor Kalmar. Gabor, it's my pleasure to introduce you to Martha Cameron and Anna Cameron. Unfortunately, they are not my wife and daughter but rather my sister-in-law and niece. I am not married."

"I am honored," the man said, putting his hand over his heart and bowing to Martha and Anna. "Allow me to introduce my daughter Edith Kalmar."

"Pleased to meet you," Edith said, glancing at them and then looking down at the floor.

I am honored. How strangely this man spoke! And to put his hand over his heart? Too funny! Anna looked at Martha, but instead of laughing at this weird man, Martha smiled at him.

"Norbert's friends are my friends too," she said, offering her hand.

Again, Gabor Kalmar bowed to them. His dark eyes shone.

A jumble of voices sounded around Anna like squawking in a startled chicken run. A woman's voice made itself audible in this noise.

"Martha," the voice said.

A tall, beautiful woman in a long blue silk dress with silver-blond hair reaching down to her waist rushed up. The bystanders moved aside and looked after her along with Norbert, his friend Gabor Kalmar, and Edith Kalmar.

"Martha." The voice of the beautiful woman seemed to fill the whole place. "What a pleasure to see you again! I have such fabulous memories of our time together at this famous academy."

"How nice to see you again, Ingrid."

"May I introduce my daughter Miriam Andersson to you?" Ingrid's voice rang again. "Miriam, come, and greet my friend Martha Cameron."

A beautiful girl, also with long silver-blond hair and violet-blue eyes, stepped in front of Martha, bowed her head, and said, "I am pleased to meet you, Mrs. Cameron."

"I am pleased too," Martha said, putting her left arm around Anna's shoulders.

“Ingrid, may I introduce my daughter Anna Cameron to you? Anna, this is Ingrid Andersson, my classmate.”

“Pleased to meet you,” Anna said.

“So, this is your daughter?” Ingrid Andersson asked. “What a lovely girl! Just a pity that she only has brown hair and not beautiful blond hair like you. Hair like her father probably? And her eyes are —look at me—her eyes are not blue like yours but green. And not exciting leaf green but rather moss green. All in all, a pretty girl.”

Anna blushed. *All in all, a pretty girl!* Who did this goat think she was? Oh, she should not insult goats. Animals were innocent. This big blond monster of a woman, however, made all these hurtful remarks even with a sweet smile! Anna gasped for air.

Beautiful Miriam stepped in front of her and offered her hand. “I’m glad to meet you, Anna.”

“Hi,” she said, shaking Miriam’s hand, which felt cold and clammy.

“I hope we become best friends, Anna.”

“I don’t need a friend,” she said.

She already had a friend, and Julius was the best friend she could wish for.

Miriam's eyes looked at her so intensely that she could hardly look away. It was strange. Suddenly the voices around her surged and swelled up and down. Her head hurt. How cold it suddenly was despite the sunshine!

"Are you alright?" Martha asked, putting her arm around her shoulders again.

Martha's arm seemed to radiate a wave of warm, golden energy that seeped through her body. She was warm again.

Three girls in cherry-red school uniforms walked past her side by side. They had remarkably long hair hanging over their backs. Two had blond hair and one black. How pretty they were! They whispered, went very close to Ingrid Andersson and said in unison, "Good morning, Mrs. Andersson." Then they disappeared into the crowd, giggling.

Anna's heart pounded faster. All the girls and boys in cherry-red school uniforms here were her new classmates. She would have lessons with these unfamiliar students day in, day out. If only Julius were here!

"Martha, Martha, there you are! I've been looking for you everywhere," a man called.

Anna looked around and saw the man pushing his way through the crowd. He was a bear of a man with short red curls, a red beard, and a face full of freckles. His blue eyes looked friendly at Martha.

“Angus, dear Angus,” Martha said, and this bear of a man put his strong arms around her and hugged her closely.

Ingrid Andersson came closer and placed her slender white hand on his arm. “What a special pleasure it is to see my classmate Angus McGregor again,” Ingrid Andersson said.

“Oh, really?” he said. “Who would have thought that? During our school days, you were constantly moaning about me.” He nodded to her and turned to Martha and Anna.

“That must be your daughter Anna, right? Good day, Anna. I'm Angus McGregor and these two … Where are they? Oh there. Come closer. So, these two are my twins, Fiona and Duncan. Hey you two, you can finally meet my school friend Martha Cameron and her daughter Anna Cameron. I'm glad you three are in the same class.”

Fiona McGregor and Duncan McGregor were freckled like their father and red-haired like their father, except that Fiona's curls were a bit longer.

And of course, the twins did not have beards! Anna could not help smiling. The twins smiled back.

"Ssh."

At that sound everyone become quieter. She turned and saw a woman in a black robe standing on the stairs to the school portal. The wind played with her blond curls. Beside her sat a black cat with golden eyes, slowly moving his tail back and forth.

Chapter 3

Welcome

The people who had been talking so enthusiastically just a moment earlier turned to the woman on the stairs and became silent. Only Norbert whispered.

"Wow!" he said quietly but still loud enough for Anna to hear.

"Dear parents, dear children," the woman in the black robe said. "Welcome to the Quentin Academy of Magical Arts and Sciences. My name is Elisabeth Roberts. I have been the director of the Quentin Academy for two years."

The director said even more, but it slipped past Anna. Where was Julius? Surely he had arrived already. His parents were always on time.

Had they decided to send him to another school?

But this was the next school! And hadn't their parents always said that the Quentin Academy was a good school? Really famous?

He had to come here. And if not...? It was bad enough to go to school, but without Julius it would be catastrophic!

On her left was Fiona and on her right Duncan. Edith was nowhere to be seen, but Miriam stood at the front of the stairs. How had she gotten there so fast? Where was Julius?

The director had stopped talking, and the crowd began to disperse. The parents turned around and headed for the corner of the building they had come from.

Martha petted her arm and said, "See you later."

She heard someone say something about refreshments in the park, but she knew that was not meant for her because she saw her new classmates lining up in pairs. Fiona and Duncan stood right in front of her. She saw Miriam hastily approaching. No, anyone but Miriam! She couldn't go to school for the first time with Miriam at her side!

Someone pushed through the crowd and stood next to her. Julius smiled at her.

"Where have you been hiding all this time?" he asked.

She rolled her eyes.

The two-headed snake of students set in motion with Julius at her side. They followed the director up the wide staircase into an entrance hall and down a long hallway that led to a big hall.

She had never seen such a splendid hall! Sunlight streamed through the large windows, and from the bright-green walls and ceiling, dozens of golden balls of light shone. At the end of the hall, she saw a podium with a long table on it and armchairs behind it. Row after row of chairs, divided into blocks, stood in the hall facing the podium.

"Over here," said a young man in a gray robe, beckoning her group forward and pointing to several chairs.

The director stood in front of the podium and smiled at them. When they all sat, she said,

"Welcome, dear students. My name is Elisabeth Roberts, and I am the director of the Quentin Academy of Magical Arts and Sciences.

"I am looking forward to the new school year of which you are now a part. First, let me tell you a little bit about what you can expect in your first year at Quentin Academy."

This time Anna really wanted to pay attention to what the director had to say.

"You will attend a basic study of three major subjects. These basic subjects are Animal Communication, Plant Communication, and the Art of Healing. Then there are electives in Art and Science.

"Possible art subjects include Carpet Weaving, Working with Wood or Stone, Music, Painting, and Storytelling.

"In the field of science, we have Mathematics and Earth sciences.

"Each of you must choose an elective, either in the arts or science area. You choose the subject that you enjoy the most.

"You have already learned to read, write, and calculate at home. Here you will learn things that you do not know yet. But mainly, you will develop and strengthen your own innate abilities. We, the teachers and the study companions, will help you. I hope that this school year will give us all pleasure."

The director smiled warmly at them.

"You've probably already noticed that you have your own carpets in the landing hall. You can fly with them by yourself. These carpets are set to have only two destinations—the Quentin Academy and your home. When you are home, you can fly to the academy, and when you are here, home.

"But now to the park and the parents. I hope they left us something to eat and drink."

As orderly as they had gone into the school, they came out just as disorderly. They did follow the director through the long corridor to the back of the building and through the large portal into the open, but everyone talked and jostled.

Ahead of Anna walked the three girls with the remarkably long hair. They pointed to Duncan and Fiona who walked ahead of them. The long-haired girls whispered and sniggered.

"Did you see them? That red hair! Red like a carrot!"

"And if that was not bad enough, they also have freckles!"

Suddenly, Anna felt very hot. How could they talk so spitefully about Fiona and Duncan! She took a quick step forward even though she did not know exactly what she planned to do. Pull those stupid girls by the hair or punch them in their backs?

Luckily, Julius grabbed her by the arm and held her back.

“We do not attack anyone from behind,” he said. “That’s not honorable.”

She clenched her fists and took a deep breath. Then she relaxed her hands.

“You’re right, Julius.”

The park stretched behind the landing site. Between the trees, tables and chairs had been set up, where parents and teachers sat and talked. To Anna, the adults in their brightly colored clothes looked like big butterflies, and the teachers in their black robes looked like blackbirds or ravens standing between them.

In the middle of the tables stood a particularly long table that held teacups, glasses, piles of plates, and baskets of cutlery. Large plates of cakes and pies sat on the table along with bowls of apples, pears, plums, blackberries, peaches, and grapes.

In between the bowls sat baskets full of walnuts and hazelnuts, pitchers of juice and water, and teapots of various teas on teapot-warmers.

She smiled. The director did not have to worry. Although some pieces were cut off from the cakes and pies, and some jugs were half empty, there was still enough for the director and the students to eat and to drink.

Where was Martha among all these people? Someone waved enthusiastically. Norbert. Of course, Norbert. He was unmistakable.

He sat at the same table as Martha, Lucius and Sophia Aquilas, Angus McGregor, and Gabor Kalmar. They talked animatedly and occasionally laughed. Unfortunately, Ingrid Andersson was also sitting at their table. She leaned back in her chair and sat silently.

That changed when Anna came closer with Julius, Fiona, Duncan, and Miriam coming up behind them.

"There are our adorable children," Ingrid Andersson said. "We have news for you! You will be so happy!"

Anna wanted to say, "Really?", but she did not want to be rude or make Martha sad.

"Glad you are here," Martha said.

Norbert got up. "What kind of drinks, cakes, and fruit may I bring you?" he asked.

"There are a few more armchairs for you here," said Angus McGregor, pulling a few chairs to the table.

When they were all sitting with juice, cake, and fruit in front of them, Anna could not wait any longer.

"What news?" she asked.

Angus McGregor smiled and said, "We have a good solution for Fiona and Duncan. They do not need to stay at school. The Aquilas family invited them to live with them."

"Why should they stay at school?"

"From our house in the mountains, it's a long way to the Quentin Academy. Fiona and Duncan would have to fly one and a half hours every day to and one and a half hours from school. We cannot expect them to do that. But the Aquilases are so hospitable that they have invited Fiona and Duncan."

"Great!" Julius said.

"Thanks," Duncan said.

"Thanks. I'm glad," Fiona said.

"Then we can meet after school," Anna said. "I only need about five minutes to go to Julius."

"And it takes me only four minutes to go to Anna," Julius said.

She punched him.

Although the others at the table were talking lively and contentedly, she felt uncomfortable, as if a cold hand wrapped around her heart.

"That's not all, is it?" she asked.

"You are right," Martha said. "Our family also has the opportunity to be hospitable, and"

"Which is exceedingly generous of you, dearest Martha," Ingrid interrupted.

"I have not made any promises yet, Ingrid. I want to talk to Henry first. But if Henry agrees, Miriam will live with us until you come back from your concert tour in Sweden."

"At the latest for the Winter Celebration," Ingrid Andersson said.

"I can't believe," Anna said at dinner, "that you are really thinking about having Miriam live here with us! Everything will change here. Our whole life! It will not be as comfortable as it is now. Or so friendly."

Henry looked at her seriously.

"If we are no longer generous and helpful, then we ourselves have changed, and for the worse."

"Do you want Miriam to stay at school day in and day out?" Martha asked.

"No, I don't want this! After all, I'm not going to be mean. But I would like it!"

That evening, Anna stopped at her mirror before going to bed and took a close look at herself. The green dress with the flowers that her grandmother Margaret had given her looked pretty.

But her hair! It was neither really straight nor really curly, just in between. And the color! It was neither blonde nor black. Just brown. She had used to always find her hair pretty, but now she was ashamed to have such ordinary hair.

Her eyes looked moss green, which was actually a nice color. She liked moss. But her eyebrows? Now that she looked at them critically, she could understand how someone would not find her eyebrows particularly pretty. Instead of being arched, they were straight. No one else in the family had such straight eyebrows like hers.

Only Julius had such eyebrows. In fact, his eyebrows were not only straight but also black like his straight hair and very thick. And if he looked at her seriously, she could almost get scared. And then there was his curved nose! A real eagle beak!

Nevertheless, she found Julius beautiful. She sighed deeply and turned around.

Chapter 4

Crystal Ceremony

As Anna woke up, she listened to the birds chirping and singing in their garden, so happy and high-spirited. A soft wind blew, and the garden seemed to breathe quietly.

"Time to get up," said her magical frog.

"Give me another five minutes."

The frog rolled his eyes. Everything was as pleasant as ever—except for school. Worse, before school even started, she already knew that she had to bring Miriam home. Here, to her house. To her parents, to Bennie, to their breakfasts and dinners together. To everything that gave her pleasure. Day after day. Who knew for how long?

She tried to relax again in her comfortable bed with the singing birds, but she could not.

When the frog said, "High time to get up," she got up quickly and went to her fresh room.

The smell of coffee again drifted in the air as she went down to the kitchen. As always, the sun filled the kitchen with its splendor. She hugged Martha and Henry and stroked Hector and Katinka. Benjamin was already in the kitchen. He ran to her and hugged her legs. She kissed him on the head.

As pleasant as breakfast was with her family, today a slight shadow hung over everything.

This time, she and Martha flew alone to the Quentin Academy. Again the landscape slid under them, but there was no dive around the Aquilas's house, for this carpet was well-behaved.

As they approached the academy, they saw carpets flying in from all directions. Luckily, the carpets were set to not collide. Her carpet circled the school landing site once before landing.

"I will meet Ingrid Andersson and the director right away to discuss Miriam's stay with us. I wish you a good start. Please remember that today you're flying home with your own carpet. That's exciting, right? And do not forget Miriam."

As if she could forget her!

Martha hugged her and walked into the landing hall with the rolled-up family carpet under her arm.

What a crowd of students! They wore school uniforms in bright colors. Some students wore orange and banana-yellow, leaf-green, sky-blue and plum-blue uniforms, and the largest of them violet uniforms. Luckily, there were also some in cherry-red uniforms. That was her class.

What a babble of voices! What a tumult!

Three tall students in plum-blue uniforms almost knocked her over.

"Sorry," one said.

The other said, "They're getting smaller every year, aren't they?"

"Real dwarfs," the third one said.

The student companion in the gray robe who had led them to their chairs yesterday shooed the students in the cherry-red uniforms into a corner.

"Wait here until I bring you in," he said. "By the way, my name is Wendelin Roth."

Once everyone was inside, they followed Wendelin Roth in a row of two into the splendid hall where they lined up against the left wall. The other students already sat in their seats.

Anna saw islands of blue and yellow, green and orange, and farther back, violet.

On the podium, the professors in black robes and the study companions in gray robes sat behind the long table. Only the director in her midst was missing from the table.

The hall again shone in the light of the golden balls, but it was not as quiet as yesterday. Today the hall hummed with many voices. Heads turned to look at Anna and the other first-year students. The crowd seemed like a large animal with hundreds of eyes watching her.

If only this were over! She looked around furtively. Julius stood with straight shoulders. Fiona chewed on her lower lip. Edith even shivered, but Miriam smiled as if she was pleased to be seen by all.

Then the director came, followed by her black cat, and took her place among the other professors.

When it was finally quiet in the great hall, the director rose and greeted professors and students for the new school year.

Then she said, "And now to you, the new class! You will be called individually by name. When you are called, come to me, and I will hang your crystals around your neck.

"These crystals have been cleansed of all extraneous influences. Over time, they will adjust to your thoughts and feelings, insights, and abilities. Their natural grid structure will be programmed by you.

"Always wear your crystal, under or over your clothes, during the day. Over time, your crystal will, if necessary, amplify your own energies.

"The Ceremony of Crystal Transfer introduces you to the professors and students, and at the same time, you will become part of the Quentin Academy of Magical Arts and Sciences."

The director got up, came down from the podium, and stopped beside a small table with a flat silver bowl with crystals in it. A professor with curly gray hair followed her and picked up a list.

"Adams, John," he read.

John, who was long and thin with sandy hair, stumbled as he went forward. The director put a silver chain with a disk-shaped, multi-faceted crystal around his neck. John sat down in the chair Wendelin Roth showed him.

Anna's heart started to beat faster.

"Andersson, Miriam."

Miriam pranced forward and bowed her head as the director put the crystal around her neck.

"Aquilas, Julius."

Julius moved quickly forward and received his crystal.

"Bertram, Lisa."

As she watched the director putting the crystal around Lisa's neck, Anna's heart pounded even faster because she was next.

"Cameron, Anna."

Just do not trip! Do not look left and right. Look straight ahead at the director. How beautiful she was! The crystal felt cool. She turned around. Wendelin Roth waved her to a chair. Then she sat.

Julius leaned forward and smiled at her. She began to breathe more steadily, and her heart calmed down.

Name after name was read out. When the last student in her class received his crystal and sat in his seat, all the others, professors and students, rose and clapped enthusiastically.

The students in the cherry-red school uniforms were now members of the Quentin Academy of Magical Arts and Sciences.

Chapter 5

First lessons

When the professors left the hall, everyone else pushed out.

"Hey, you red ones! Follow me!" Wendelin Roth called.

Julius grabbed Anna's hand, and she held Fiona's hand to keep them together in the crowd. With a group of other students, they ran up the stairs behind Wendelin Roth. The stream split left and right, but they followed Wendelin Roth farther and farther to the right past an open door and then into a room with a missing back wall. No, it was not missing. It was a clear glass wall through which they could look at the park.

A long desk with an armchair behind it stood against the right wall, facing two semicircular rows of four-seat tables, three in the front and five in the back.

"Oh, how beautiful this is," Anna said. "This table here is still free. Come, let's sit here."

She drew Julius and Fiona to the front four-seat table at the glass wall. The three sat down.

"Isn't this spot great? From here we can see the trees down there and the clouds in the sky. And we're also very close to the professor's desk and can see exactly what he is doing."

Some of their classmates sat down too, while others looked around. Duncan leisurely came over and sat down next to Fiona.

The three long-haired girls sat down at the front middle table next to them. As Miriam came in, she hurried to the table where Anna sat with Julius, Fiona, and Duncan.

"I can't tell you how disappointed I am that you did not wait for me, Anna," Miriam said in such a loud voice that some students turned to look at them.

"I looked for you everywhere. You had to know I wanted to sit next to you."

Then Miriam turned to Fiona. "Surely you don't mind sitting somewhere else, do you? There are still places left at the back."

"Yes, for you," Julius said.

One of the long-haired girls turned to Miriam. "You're the daughter of the singer Ingrid Andersson, right? Come sit with us. We have a place reserved for you."

Miriam looked at Anna for a few more seconds before sitting down with the long-haired ones.

Anna shook her head. What was going on in Miriam's head? She was disappointed in her? And Fiona should sit somewhere else? What a jerk! She would have liked to tell her off, but she could not.

Miriam would be living with them from now on. At home, it had always been friendly and cozy, and she did not want to destroy that with her anger. She clenched her fists and took a deep breath to calm herself.

Then Edith came to their table with tears in her eyes. The braid over her shoulder was half undone.

"I don't know where to sit."

"Oh, poor you," said Fiona.

Anna got up and looked around searchingly.

"What are you looking for?" Julius asked.

"For a chair that we can put at our table."

"That won't work," Duncan said. "These are tables for four."

He also looked around. "There must still be a good seat open."

"I already know where. Come on, Edith."

Julius got up and pulled Edith by the sleeve to the table at the back left of the wall where John Adams sat all by himself.

"Is it okay with you if Edith sits next to you?"

"Sure," said John, adjusting a chair for her.

Wendelin Roth clapped his hands.

"I hope you all have found a place by now. When Professor Angelo comes in, please get up and say, 'Good morning, Professor Angelo,' and when Professor Angelo has said good morning, you sit down again, okay?"

The door opened and a young woman in a gray robe came in and cast a shy glance at the class. She carried a flowerpot with a small tree in it. Everyone got up and said, "Good morning, Professor Angelo."

"You can sit down again," Wendelin Roth said. "Greta Sourwell here is not a professor, as you can see by her gray robe, but a study companion like me."

Embarrassed, they sat down. Greta Sourwell placed the flower pot on the long desk and stood next to Wendelin Roth in front of the glass wall.

The two study companions looked nice and so different from each other. Still, the tall Wendelin Roth—with his thick brown curls and his "Hey, follow me!"—and the shy Greta Sourwell with her smooth, blond hair seemed to get along well.

Then the door opened again and a small woman with short black curls came in quickly. This had to be the professor because she wore a black robe.

The students jumped up and said, "Good morning, Professor Angelo."

The professor stopped in front of them and looked at them one by one with her dark eyes.

She looked like a lively black sparrow and was barely taller than Anna.

"Good Morning."

The class sat down.

"My name is Amanda Angelo, and I will be teaching you plant communication. Furthermore, I am your homeroom teacher. If you have something important to discuss, you can contact me.

"Next Saturday, the Animal Festival will be celebrated all over the country, including here at the Quentin Academy, where we will show our gratitude and appreciation to the animals that live with us and also to the animals that live in nature.

"For this event, families will bring the young dogs and cats that were born this year and introduce you to them. In this way, you will find your animal companion.

"Your parents have already been invited. They will come with you to the Quentin Academy. It will be a wonderful day for all of us and an important day in your life."

There was a knock. Wendelin Roth hurried to the door and opened it. A little boy with black curly hair stood there. He wore a sherry-red school uniform.

"I'm lost," he said softly.

"Now you've found us," said Professor Angelo.

"There are still free seats in the back. And now, please introduce yourselves. Please stand up one after the other and say your name and then sit down again. We'll start in the front left here and continue to the back right."

No one could remember so many names! Still, Anna leaned forward as the long-haired girls rose in turn.

“Melanie Pratt.”

“Cordula Miller.”

“Miriam Andersson.”

“Carla Rossi.”

That was the black-haired one.

And last in the class to introduce themselves were:

“Juan Martinez.”

“Edith Kalmar.”

“John Adams.”

“Before we start plant communication, I‘d like to ask you to think about which elective you want to study,” said Professor Angelo. “Please think about it when you go home and inform Wendelin Roth of your choice in two days.

“Now to plant communication. What kind of plant is this? Duncan McGregor?”

“A tree.”

“Correct. A conifer or a deciduous tree? Melanie Pratt?”

“A conifer.”

Had Professor Angelo already learned all their names?

“Correct. What tree in particular?”

Professor Angelo looked around the students, searching.

“Raise your hand, if you think you know it.”

Edith hesitantly raised her hand.

“Well?”

“A spruce.”

“Right, if a little quietly said. This is a special spruce, a blue spruce.

“The first step is taken. We know what kind of plant this is. Now let’s start with the communication.

“Close your eyes and feel your feet in your socks and shoes. Breathe in and out slowly. Good.

“Now send your attention to the spruce on my desk as if sending out a thread of consciousness. Be completely still in your mind. Listen. Feel.”

Anna could feel her feet and her breath, but her thoughts were like frightened chickens running around in her head. And she kept hearing Miriam say,

"I cannot tell you how disappointed I am."

Back to the tree. She could do it at home. At home, she could feel the energies of Henry's oak and Martha's maple tree. Why could she not feel the energies of the spruce now?

Could she at least see the spruce image in her mind? No. Again and again Miriam's blue eyes came to the fore.

"Open your eyes. What impressions did you receive? What feelings?" Professor Angelo asked.

The class was silent.

"Well? Nothing at all? Carla Rossi?"

"Something pointed?"

"Stefan Winter?"

"Like the sea?"

"Hmm, interesting. No one else? Then we will do it again. Close your eyes. Feel your feet. Slow your breath. Don't think. Send a thread of awareness to this tree here. Very quiet. Listen. Feel."

Minutes passed as Professor Angelo watched the students try to calm down and listen. Some closed their eyes. Others frowned. Still others clenched their fists. Lisa Bertram seemed to hold her breath. Carla Rossi rubbed her forehead. John Adam dropped his head forward as if he had fallen asleep.

Anna tried to calm her thoughts, but again and again Miriam came to her mind.

After a while, she heard Professor Angelo say,

"Open your eyes. What kind of impressions did you get? Oliver Campbell?"

"Cold?"

"Cordula Müller?"

"Something hard."

"John Adams?"

"Pleasant, just pleasant."

"Pretty good. Edith Kalmar?"

"I don't know. Something like peace?"

"Yes, you do know it. Peace. Correct."

Professor Angelo gently ran her hand over the little spruce.

"That's a start. Tomorrow we will meet for the first hour at the greenhouses."

With energetic steps, she left the classroom. Greta Sourwell followed her with the tree, and Wendelin Roth said,

"All of you follow me."

Chapter 6

How do you fly these carpets?

Wendelin Roth went outside in front of them and stopped in the middle of the landing site. The students of Class One gathered around him like chicks around a hen.

He looked at a list and ran his hand through his brown curls.

"Hey, you! Julius Aquilas, Fiona, Duncan McGregor, Anna Cameron, and Miriam Andersson, wait here until I have time for you. You are special cases because you will receive new carpets afterwards. However, in the meantime, you can watch how the others learn how to handle their carpets.

"You others, please follow Greta Sourwell, Tim Brown, and Manfred Erler into the landing hall. They will help you find your carpets."

Greta Sourwell and the other study companions waved for the students to follow them.

Anna heard voices sound out of the hall.

“Look for your name tags. They are arranged alphabetically.”

“How do you get up there? Stand here on the platform and press the red button several times if you want to go higher or the blue button if you want to go down again.”

“Don’t be scared. You can hold on to the railing.”

“How do you unroll them carpet? We’ll do that together outside.”

One by one, the students came out of the hall with their rolled carpets under their arms.

“Spread out. Make room for each other,” Wendelin Roth said.

“And now please put your carpets on the floor and look for your name on the side. Do you see it?”

It took a while for everyone to find a suitable place for their carpets and then to find their names on the carpets.

“And now press on your name.”

The carpets rolled out.

“Now you can sit on your carpets.”

“What if my carpet just flies off?”

“It won’t. It’s programmed not to do that. Also, no carpet will fly even an inch if the force field is not turned on.”

“How do I turn it on?” Lisa Bertram asked.

“At the edge of your carpet, near your name, are two stripes. Do you see them? The red stripe is for the force field, and the blue stripe is for the temperature. But first to the force field. If you rub the red stripe, the force field will turn on. Give it a try.”

Like flickering half soap bubbles, the force fields appeared around the carpets. The force fields only reached down to the ground.

“Why does the carpet have a force field? So that I don’t fall off?”

“Correct. It also prevents you from colliding with trees, houses, or other carpets. The force field also protects you from rain, hail, and snow.

“At the same time, it allows in a gentle stream of air so you can breathe. This air is immediately heated to a temperature of 23° Celsius.

“If that’s too warm or too cold for you, you can push the blue stripe forward then it’ll get warmer, or push back, and it’ll get colder. Please try this out.”

Anna watched the students of Class One try out the blue stripe on their rugs, pushing it back and forth. Suddenly, the usually pale John Adams looked flushed. Sweat droplets appeared on his forehead. He quickly pushed the blue stripe backwards.

“And now how do I start the carpet?” Melanie Pratt, one of the long-haired girls, asked.

“By telling it. But don’t do that yet. Please turn off the force field for a moment. As Professor Roberts said to you in the Great Hall, with these carpets you can only fly to two places—from here to home and from your house to the Quentin Academy.

“If you want to fly home after school, just say ‘home’ and the carpet will fly you home.”

“How does the carpet know where my house is?”

“This information is linked to your name on the carpet. Are there any other questions? No? Good. Who wants to be the first to fly home alone? Lisa Bertram? Then get started.”

Lisa sat down on her rug, stroking the short brown hair from her round face, took a deep breath, and said, “Home.”

Nothing happened.

"You have yet to switch on the force field," Wendelin Roth sighed softly.

Lisa switched on the force field and said, "Home."

The carpet took off, and the students on the landing site clapped enthusiastically.

"Who wants to leave next?"

Successively, the students flew off, and the ever-shrinking number of students on the landing site clapped. Then, apart from Anna's group, only Edith was left. She sat on her carpet and cried.

"Oh, my goodness," Fiona said.

"What's wrong, Edith Kalmar?" Wendelin Roth asked. "Don't you want to fly home?"

"Yes, but I don't understand everything you said."

"But it's easy."

He ran his hand through his curly hair again, which became more and more tousled.

"Shall I explain it to you again?"

"I know what you said, but what if it doesn't work for me?"

He looked at Greta Sourwell—the other student companions had already left—and Greta Sourwell looked back at him. Her face, which had been so rosy before, was now pale.

"You will manage, Edith," Duncan said.

"Yes, don't worry. You will fly home in a moment," Julius said. "We will find a solution."

"May I fly with Edith?" Anna asked Wendelin Roth. "Together we can do it. Right, Edith?"

Edith nodded.

"And how are you going to come back?" Wendelin Roth asked.

"First, we both fly to her house to see if she can do it. And then she'll bring me back and fly home alone."

"That could work. Is that okay with you, Edith Kalmar?"

Edith nodded again. She even smiled.

"But turn right back, yes? Don't dawdle. Can I rely on you?"

"Yes, Mr. Roth."

"You can call me Wendelin Roth. So, let's go!"

Anna sat down on Edith's carpet. Edith switched on the force field, said "home," and the carpet flew off.

"Hui," said Anna. "We're flying, Edith! We're flying by ourselves! You can do it! Hooray, we're flying!"

"Maybe I really can do it."

"Of course, you can. Otherwise, we would not be up here. And this is all there is to it. Isn't that great? The carpet flies by itself. How beautiful our school looks from up here!"

Woodlands, houses, and meadows spread below them and slipped away from under them. In the distance, Anna saw a river to which the carpet seemed to fly. A house surrounded by tall trees on a flat hill came closer.

"Is that your house? Yes? Looks comfortable. Are those horses over there?"

The carpet landed on a lawn behind the house.

"Welcome to our home," Edith said, switching off the force field.

A woman in a white blouse with puffy sleeves and a short, wide, colorful skirt come out of the house towards them. A long black braid hung over her right shoulder.

“Welcome,” said the woman.

“Mama!”

Edith ran to her mother and hugged her.

“My dear Edith, you did it! You flew home and even brought along a school friend.”

Edith’s mother turned to Anna. “Welcome to the Kalmars! I am Julianna Kalmar.”

“Hello, Mrs. Kalmar, I am Anna Cameron.”

“Anna Cameron, it’s an honor. I’ve heard a lot about you.”

Julianna Kalmar put her hand over her heart and briefly bowed her head.

“I am pleased to invite you into our house. I just took an apple pie out of the oven. May I interest you in a slice?”

“Thank you for the invitation, Mrs. Kalmar, but we have promised to return immediately. Edith will bring me back to the academy and then fly home alone.”

Julianna Kalmar nodded.

"That's a good plan. Thank you for accompanying Edith on her first flight. Please, visit us again and a little longer than today."

They smiled at each other.

When Anna and Edith arrived back at the landing site, they were greeted enthusiastically.

"I'm relieved to see you back so soon," Wendelin Roth said.

"Well done," said Julius.

"I knew you could do it, Edith," Fiona said.

Duncan grinned at Edith. "Of course, she can."

"Do you dare to fly home alone?" Wendelin Roth asked.

"Yes," Edith said. "I can do it now."

"I met Mrs. Kalmar. She invited me to visit her," Anna said. She felt herself glow with joy. "They have horses in the pasture."

"Here we have our beloved Anna back." Miriam leaned in close to Anna. "Do you always have to be the best?" she added softly, looking intensely at her with her blue eyes.

Anna shivered. She crossed her arms. How cold it suddenly was!

She waved to Edith as she left, then followed Wendelin Roth, who led them to their new carpets. Her small carpet was exchanged for a larger one, which also bore the name *Cameron, Anna*.

Miriam's carpet remained in the landing hall, as did Fiona and Duncan's large carpets, in case they wanted to fly home on weekends. Julius got an even bigger carpet than Anna because the three of them would all fly with it.

"See you tomorrow!"

They waved to each other. Why did everything feel so far away? Anna sat down next to Miriam on the carpet on which Wendelin Roth had placed Miriam's suitcase.

"I will fly," Miriam said.

"I don't care."

Miriam babbled something, but Anna did not listen. The carpet flew over Oakville and over the now familiar woodlands and meadows. There was the Aquilases' house, there the brook, and here her house. Why couldn't she be happy? Why was she so cold?

When the carpet landed behind her house, Miriam turned off the force field.

Martha, who knelt between the flowerbeds, straightened up, brushed dirt from her green dress, and smiled as she met them.

"Martha! Oh, Martha!" Anna hugged her mother tightly, and suddenly she felt warm and happy again.

"Welcome, Miriam," Martha said.

"Anna! Anna!"

Benjamin came running and snuggled against her. Katinka came, then Hector, and finally Henry came from his workshop. He smiled friendly.

"Congratulations on your first solo flight," he said.

"Mrs. Cameron and Mr. Cameron, I am so infinitely grateful to you for letting me live with you in your beautiful house for a few weeks!"

Anna rolled her eyes. Beautiful house! She had not even seen it!

"Let's go into the house first and have a cup of tea," Henry said. "Then we can discuss everything."

Chapter 7

An evening with Miriam

Anna stayed in the garden for a moment, watching the others go inside. Martha opened the door, and Miriam walked in first. Katinka followed Martha. Hector went tail-wagging beside Henry, who carried Miriam's suitcase. Benjamin, however, stopped beside her and looked at her.

"Don't you want to go inside, Bennie?"

"I stay with you."

"I'm going into the house in a moment. I just want to stay here in the garden for a while. The flowers and herbs smell so sweet. You go ahead inside. I'll be coming soon."

He took her hand. "I stay with you."

"All right, let's go together."

Now the kitchen was not lit by the morning light, but by the evening sun that shone through the glass door that led to the living room.

Henry prepared tea, and Martha put plates and cups on the table. Today they were as blue as the bright autumn sky outside.

The kitchen was beautiful as always, but not as comfortable. Miriam was there talking.

“There’s the adorable little boy I just saw. He’s so cute, and what beautiful blond curls he has. Come here. What’s your name?”

Benjamin did not come and did not answer. He stayed beside Anna.

“Don’t you want to say good day to Miriam?” Henry asked.

Benjamin remained silent. Miriam approached him and held out her arms to him. The little boy hid behind his sister.

“Miriam, may I ask you to sit down here?” Martha said. “Once Bennie gets used to your presence, he’ll certainly talk to you.”

Anna gently stroked Benjamin’s head. She completely understood him not wanting to go to Miriam.

The tea was refreshing, and the plum cake tasted good. It would have been almost comfortable at the afternoon tea, if Miriam had not kept talking. Could she never shut up?

"Your kitchen is so elegant. And you have so many interesting devices here. And those stylish cups and plates are such a special blue."

"I'm glad you like our kitchen," Henry said. "After tea, we'll go upstairs and show you the room we have designated for you."

Anna had not thought of that yet. Which room? Hopefully not the guest room next to her room. She did not want to sleep so close to Miriam.

When they all went upstairs, she was glad that Henry led Miriam to a room facing her room, at least separated from her room by the corridor. But before they went in, Miriam ran to a door at the end of the hall, which was slightly open. Miriam opened it wide and went inside.

"What a fantastic room. This is the most beautiful room I have ever seen. And this big bed is a real four-poster bed. And the blankets are silk. Are the waves moving in the pictures? I have never seen such pictures. And this carpet—it's as if the flowers on it are alive. Just beautiful, the entire room."

Anna also thought the room was beautiful. It was where Martha's parents lived when they came to visit.

"If I could live in this fantastic room, I would be the happiest person in the world. May I live here, please?"

It felt as if her heart had stopped. Miriam living in this very special room? In Margaret's and John's room? Her sleeping in the bed where Anna's fine and dear grandparents usually slept?

"I am afraid that you'll have to settle for being the second happiest person in the world," Henry said, "because this room is reserved for the grandparents Summerfield. I hope you will be happy in the room we have intended for you."

Miriam did not seem to listen.

"Oh, is that a sound-light organ? My mother has one too. I love to play this organ. Of course, I do not play as well as my mother does. Who can do that? May I?"

Without waiting for an answer, Miriam sat down in front of the organ and played a simple melody. Waves of dull yellow light spread through the room.

"Since you enjoy playing this organ, we'll bring it down to the living room so you can play it anytime," Martha said.

When Miriam got up and followed Martha into the room intended for her, Benjamin stood in front of the organ and pressed the keys with both hands. He made a jarring sound and triangular and square patterns in poppy-red and leaf-green light appeared around the organ.

"Henry, why does the organ sound so different now and makes different patterns of light than before?" Anna asked.

"The sound-light organ not only plays the notes associated with the keys, but it also responds to the energies of the person playing it."

"And Bennie has a triangular and square energy?"

"Bennie has not yet learned to play tunes. He presses random keys. You can hear that from the sounds, and you can see that in the shapes of the light patterns, but the colors themselves are clear and beautiful, are they not?"

She nodded. Yes, Bennie had to have good energies if he could produce such colors. She took Benjamin by the hand and followed Henry into Miriam's room. Miriam's room was the same size as her room and furnished almost exactly like hers. The bed was not a four-poster bed as in her grandparents' room, but it was comfortable enough.

"Anna's room is opposite," Henry said, putting down Miriam's suitcase.

"When you have refreshed and changed, come down, yes?" Martha said.

Anna heaved a sigh as she entered her room.

She quickly took off her clothes and put them in the refresher. Then she went into the freshroom, set it to lavender scent and a warm temperature, and let the air flow wash around her with purifying energies. She stayed there for a long time, because there was a lot to rinse off.

The dress that she put on had been a gift from Margaret. It was a short dress, dark green with lavender aster flowers. She looked at herself in the mirror and thought she looked pretty.

Suddenly the door opened behind her, and Miriam stood in the room.

"What are you thinking just barging in here? Can't you knock?"

“Why does it matter? Do you have something to hide?”

“Never come into my room again if I have not said ‘Come in.’ Never again.”

As if she had heard nothing, Miriam went through Anna’s room and looked at the pictures on the walls.

Anna looked at Miriam. She wore a light blue silk dress with a dark blue velvet belt. Her silver-blond hair reached down to her hips. Her eyes were violet blue and her features fine and even. She should have looked like a fairytale princess, but something was missing that would have made her really beautiful. What was it?

“That must be the same painter who painted the pictures of the sea. Such beautiful colors, and the branches of the tree are moving in the wind,” Miriam said.

She had to admit that Miriam had good taste indeed.

“My grandfather John painted them.”

“Oh my God! There’s a frog sitting on your bed.”

“So what?”

Miriam took a step back. “Is it poisonous?”

Anna wanted to say he was very toxic, but she did not want to lie.

“That is my magic frog. He wakes me up in the morning.”

She went to the bed and petted her frog.

“The frog wakes you up? How does he do that?”

“He says, ‘Good morning. Time to get up.’”

“He says it? He can speak? May I touch him?”

“No. Don’t touch him. Hands off.”

Miriam stopped and looked into Anna’s eyes. Then she took a few steps to the window, turned around quickly, and reached for the frog. Anna was faster and took him in both hands.

“I just wanted to see if you’re serious about the frog,” Miriam said. She went to the window. “I also have such a comfortably wide windowsill in my room.”

She sat and looked down into the garden. “What is Benjamin doing down there?”

“Bennie?”

Anna sat next to her and looked down as well. She saw her little brother eagerly digging a hole in the soft earth between the asters with a flat stone.

“He did that three days ago too. He pretends to be a squirrel.”

“A squirrel?”

“Yes, he makes holes in the ground and then he puts in nuts, like the squirrels do. Come on, let’s go down. Martha is waiting for us.”

While Anna helped Bennie dig, Martha led Miriam through the garden, showing her Henry’s workshop, her herb kitchen, and then the living room where the sound-light organ already stood.

At dinner, Miriam said, “I can’t get over you refusing to lend me your frog, Anna. I did not think you were that selfish.”

“No, you can’t have my frog.”

“Only for one night, please. I want so much to hear the frog saying good morning to me.”

“Tell yourself, good morning.”

“Anna!”

Henry and Martha looked at her.

“What’s up with you today?” Henry asked.

“Please, Mr. Cameron, don’t be angry with Anna. I am so grateful to you both for your generous hospitality. It was wrong of me to expect such hospitality from Anna too. I’m sorry.”

Silence spread.

After a while, Miriam asked, “May I thank you for the tasty dinner by playing a song?”

Martha and Henry nodded.

“What is Benjamin’s favorite song?”

“‘Good Evening, Good Night.’”

Miriam sat down at the organ while the Cameron family settled on the sofas in the living room, Benjamin on Martha’s lap.

Anna wished herself far away. There had never been such an uncomfortable silence in this house. She hardly dared to look at her parents.

When Miriam sang “Good evening, good night” and played on the organ, murky blue and gray color waves filled the room. Blurred tones accompanied Miriam’s clear voice.

Benjamin slid off Martha’s lap, went into the kitchen, and rattled around in there.

Anna looked at Martha and Henry. Did they like the concert? Did they not notice that something was false here?

Chapter 8

Tree Companions

The sun rose. Birds twittered. Raindrops sparkled on the leaves of the walnut tree. The troubled dreams of the night faded with the morning splendor. Anna sat on the windowsill and deeply breathed in the fresh air.

"Good morning," the frog said. "Time to get up."

"You ninny, I've been up a long time."

She went to her bed and stroked the frog. In the fresh room she chose chamomile, temperature warm and air flow medium. How soothing that was.

Then she got her clothes out of the refresher and put them on. Actually, a school uniform was quite practical. She did not have to think about what to wear in the morning and was always well-dressed.

When she came into the kitchen and saw Martha and Henry, she hesitated. After the frosty mood last night, she did not really know what to say and do. She had never felt so uncomfortable at home before.

Hector came tail-wagging toward her and sniffed at her. Henry, who had looked out the window, turned back towards her.

"Good morning, Anna."

"Good morning," she said in a low voice.

"Good morning." Martha smiled at her. "Today we're having cereal. Would you like coffee or tea?"

"Tea, please. How can I help you?"

"Breakfast is ready. We're just waiting for Miriam."

Anna crouched down next to Benjamin, who sat on the floor playing with Katinka. He rolled a hazelnut in her direction, and the black and white cat rolled it back to him.

"Anna," he said, wrapping his arms around her.

She kissed him on the head.

After a while, Miriam joined them.

"A wonderful morning to you, Mrs. Cameron, and to you, Mr. Cameron. There's our cute little Benjamin. Come, Benjamin. Sit down with me."

Benjamin rolled the nut in Katinka's direction. Katinka rolled it back

"Benjamin, come here."

When he did not come, Miriam approached him.

He clung to Anna. "No, no."

"It's best that you sit in between Mama and me. You like that, Bennie, don't you?"

Henry picked him up and put him on the chair.

The cereal with apples and nuts tasted good, as did the tea. If only Miriam did not talk all the time!

Finally, it was time to fly to school. Miriam switched on the force field, and the carpet took off. As they flew over the Quentin Academy, Anna saw a group of students in red school uniforms standing near the right wing. Those had to be the greenhouses.

As soon as they landed, Miriam headed for her new friends. They whispered and looked over at Anna. Melanie Pratt shook her head.

Anna pressed her hand on the edge of the carpet, and the carpet rolled tight. She carried it into the landing hall. There, under the sign "Cameron, Anna," Julius, Duncan, Fiona, and Edith stood smiling at her. Together, they went to the greenhouses.

“Everything alright?” Julius asked softly. No, nothing was alright. He must have felt it. He knew her so well!

“I’ll tell you later.”

“Hello, Class One,” Wendelin Roth said. “Come along this way.”

She led them into one of the greenhouses. The air was humid and warm and smelt of earth.

There were transparent shelves on the glass windows and dozens of flower pots with small trees in them on those shelves. The flower pots had two small plaques. One of the plaques had the kind of tree written on it, and the other one was blank.

“Listen, everybody,” Wendelin Roth said, waving a list. “Please tell me which electives you have chosen.”

Anna had known for a long time what kind of elective subject she wanted to take: storytelling. Grandmother Margaret could tell stories so wonderfully that everyone listened with enthusiasm. Her stories were so vivid they were like experiencing the adventures firsthand. That was what Anna wanted to learn.

She looked around curiously and listened to what the others had chosen for electives. Julius and Duncan chose Earth sciences.

Fiona chose carpet weaving. “Then I’ll be able to weave along with my mother,” she said. “I already enjoy just watching her.”

John Adams and Juan Martinez selected Earth sciences, Alexander Orlow and Lisa Bertram chose mathematics, and Miriam music, of course.

Just as Wendelin Roth had finished writing everyone’s chosen subjects on his list, the door of the greenhouse opened, and Professor Angelo came in, followed by Greta Sourwell.

“Good morning, Professor Angelo,” the class said in unison.

“Good Morning,” Professor Angelo said. “Today you will find your tree companion, the tree that will one day grow in your garden and accompany you on your life’s journey. You will know which tree that is. Go slowly past these trees, and if you like one of them very much, take it and sit down on one of those chairs.”

Professor Angelo pointed to the chairs arranged in a semicircle in the center of the greenhouse.

The students of Class One looked around and then walked slowly past the shelves with the small trees, stopped, walked on, and stopped again. Every now and then a student took a tree and sat down.

"I don't prefer any of them," John Adams said. "I think they're all pretty nice."

"Do not just look with your eyes, John Adams," Professor Angelo said. "It's more about the feeling."

The long-haired girls went together in a group and whispered with each other. Melanie Pratt repeated softly, "It's more about the feeling." They snorted.

Professor Angelo turned to them. "Melanie Pratt, Cordula Müller, Miriam Andersson, and Carla Rossi, you are new to this academy and apparently do not know how to behave yourselves. Today I want to overlook your disrespect. Tomorrow, no longer."

The long-haired girls fell silent and did not look at each other.

Anna went back along the shelves. Most students had by now found their trees and sat with them in the chairs. Duncan held a white oak in his hands, Julius a cedar, Fiona a beech, Edith a blue spruce, and Miriam a magnolia. Even John had finally decided on a walnut tree, but Anna was still undecided.

“It looks as if you’re being dragged between two trees, Anna Cameron,” Professor Angelo said. “Which are they?”

“The linden tree and the red oak.”

“Interesting,” Professor Angelo said, looking at her searchingly. “Two very different energies. Which tree feels right for you?”

“The red oak,” Anna said, taking it off the shelf.

“Good choice.”

Professor Angelo sat down in one of the chairs in the semicircle. Wendelin Roth and Greta Sourwell sat to the left and right of her.

“Duncan McGregor, sit down on this chair here in the middle so that everyone can see your tree, a white oak,” Professor Angelo said. “And you, students of Class One, look at the tree with your eyes open or closed. Feel toward the tree with the expectation that you will recognize its peculiarity.

“Each tree species has a characteristic feature. You should now learn to perceive these. Do your best to keep your mind calm.”

Earlier, Anna could. In the past, life was good too. There used to be no frosty silence at home, and when she came to the kitchen, she could be sure she was welcome. She had not been so beastly before, but since Miriam's arrival, everything was different.

Calm. Calm. What did she feel when she concentrated on Duncan's tree? An impression formed in her mind, something like strength. Or defiance. No, steadfastness. Was that the energy of the tree or of Duncan? Or of both?

Then Miriam's image came to her mind, and the impression of the tree blurred. It was probably just a fantasy.

"Who wants to share their impression with us?" Professor Angelo asked.

Silence.

"Juan Martinez, do you have something to share with us?"

"No. I'm sorry, Professor Angelo."

"Lisa Bertram, what's your impression?"

"Ah, none at all. I need more time."

"Alexander Orlow, what did you perceive?"

"Nothing specific, Professor Angelo. I'm sorry."

"Miriam Andersson, can you share an impression with us?"

"Yes, of course. My impression is of something very special, rare. Something that you would like to have more of. An impression of a very extraordinary tree—"

Professor Angelo interrupted her. "Miriam Andersson, you are blathering. On one point, you're right. This energy is something special. That is steadfastness."

Anna smiled. Her fleeting impression of Duncan's tree had been correct after all. Too bad that the impression had dissolved so quickly.

"Can anyone tell me why Duncan McGregor has chosen this tree?"

This time there was a voluntary answer. Edith raised her hand.

"Well, Edith Kalmar?"

"Because he himself has this quality?"

"Correct. The trees you have chosen have attracted you because you share a major quality with them. Duncan McGregor, you can retreat back into the semicircle.

"Now please, John Adams, sit in the chair in the center. You others, do your best to perceive the energy of his tree, a walnut tree. By now you have an inkling of how to go about it."

When Professor Angelo asked the class after a few minutes, several students raised their hands.

"Yes, Stefan Winter?"

"Something positive. Something quite positive."

"Carla Rossi?"

"Strong communication, Professor Angelo."

"And you, Fiona McGregor?"

"Openness, Professor Angelo."

"Pretty good. You will learn this over time. The main feature of the walnut tree is the energy to speak from the heart. Of course, trees communicate very differently from humans, but people with this energy often speak from the heart. John Adams, you can sit back in the semicircle.

"Now to you, Class One. Wendelin Roth and Greta Sourwell will soon help you to put your name on the plaque of your tree's pot.

"Your trees stay here in the greenhouse. At the end of the school year, you will take them home and plant them there. The day after tomorrow, we will meet again at the usual hour."

With energetic steps, the little professor with the black curls left the greenhouse.

As they flew over Oakville, Anna thought about how interesting the main characteristics of the trees were. What were the main characteristic of a linden tree? And especially of a red oak? Or of Julius's cedar?

"You did it again!"

She jumped. "Did what?"

"You always have to have it better than everyone else. Now you're also the teacher's favorite."

"What do you mean by that?"

"My friends and I, we just laugh a bit and are getting snarled at for it. And you dawdle around and delay everyone, and supposedly you can't decide on a tree, but Professor Angelo talks to you in the friendliest way. I'll find out how you do it."

Anna took a deep breath. "Just leave me alone."

Chapter 9

The frog

It started to rain when they landed at home. Benjamin came running towards her crying.

Anna knelt down and took him in her arms. “Bennie, what’s going on? Did you hurt yourself?”

“The fro-frog is dead,” he said, sobbing.

“What?”

“The frog is dead.”

He cried harder. Henry and Martha hurried toward her.

“I’m so sorry,” Martha said.

“Beanie recently found your frog under your window. Unfortunately, totally shattered,” Henry said.

“My frog is shattered?”

It began raining harder.

“Come on. Let’s go inside,” Martha said. “We can continue talking in there.”

Continue talking? What was there to talk about? Her frog was shattered. Her dear frog.

Nevertheless, she followed the others into the house. Martha poured strong black tea for everyone except Benjamin.

“Take a lot of sugar, Anna,” she said, pulling the sugar pot closer.

“Henry, can you mend my frog?” Anna asked.

“Of course, I’ll do my best to mend him. Unfortunately, after my first inventory I have to say that I have to replace almost all the components. Also, your frog needs a new housing ... “

“Now it really sounds like my frog is dead. ‘Components,’ ‘housing’... My frog is more than components. He is special, as if he were alive. He looks so cute when he rolls his eyes, and he croaks so nicely when he says good morning.”

Whether she wanted to or not, she had to cry again like Benjamin, who now sat on Martha’s lap.

“I’m sorry that I expressed myself so technically,” Henry said. “I apologize.”

Miriam, who had been silent up until now, burst out with her comment.

"Anna, don't make a fuss," she said. "You act as if someone has died."

Did Miriam have no feeling?

"Looking at the situation from several angles," Henry said, "the frog is partly mechanical and partly energetic—a bounded artificial intelligence. You're right, Anna. Your frog is special."

Martha put her hand on Anna's arm. How wonderful it was to feel that good, warming energy. Only then did Anna realize how cold she had become.

They sat in silence for a while then Henry took Bennie to his workshop. Martha went into her herbal kitchen, and Miriam played the organ. Anna went to her room and lay down on the bed beside the pillow her frog should be sitting on and wept. After a while, she calmed down a bit.

In the freshroom, she was aware of a thought that had been waiting to be noticed by her all along. How did the frog get outside? He could not jump after all. Someone must have thrown him down. But who?

She put on the darkest, dreariest clothes she had—a pair of black trousers with a dark green tunic over them.

It was warm in the kitchen. Golden balls of light illuminated the room. The rain still clapped on the window panes.

The vegetable peeler peeled potatoes and carrots, and the vegetable slicer cut the leek into small pieces. Martha washed herbs for the vegetable soup, and Katinka lolled in her basket.

It was so peaceful in the kitchen that Anna did not want to ask the question that burned on her tongue. Who threw the frog out of the window?

Instead she remained silent and set the table. Martha poured the vegetables into the saucepan on the stove and added the herbs, water and butter. Soon, the ingredients simmered in the pot and an aromatic scent moved through the kitchen.

"I have a hunch that there will be food soon," Henry said with a wink as he came in from the downpour of rain with Benjamin in his arms and Hector beside him.

Hector shook himself, and Martha dried Benjamin's head. Miriam came down the stairs in a pink silk dress and sat down at their table.

As they started to eat, Benjamin brought his hand forward, which he had been holding behind his back the whole time.

"For you, Anna," he said, handing her his magic toy mouse.

"Oh, Bennie."

Anna had to cry again.

"You don't like the mouse?" Benjamin asked.

"Yes, I do, Bennie. I really like the mouse. Thank you! After dinner we'll play with it in the kitchen, yes?"

"Another magical toy?" Miriam asked. "The children in this family are really spoiled."

"And yet someone threw my frog out the window. Who was that?"

Before Henry and Martha could recover from the horror of this sudden question, Miriam quickly said, "That's obvious. Benjamin did it. Right, Benjamin? You didn't mean to do it. You just wanted to play with the frog on the windowsill, and then it fell out the window."

Miriam looked intensely at the little boy with her violet-blue eyes.

Benjamin looked back defiantly.

"No, he did not. We asked him immediately," Henry said.

"Do you think he's telling you the truth?"

"Of course."

"Oh, so it was you, Anna. You put the frog on the windowsill this morning and then leaned out of the window and accidentally knocked the frog down. Such things can happen, right, Anna?"

Miriam's eyes looked at her intensely. It seemed to Anna as if Miriam's eyes were getting bigger and bigger, and her voice sounded like an echo.

"No. I don't know. Maybe."

Her head throbbed. She fell off the chair.

When she came to, she lay on a sofa in the living room, and Martha lifted her head a bit. She held out a cup of herbal tea to her mouth.

"Drink," she said. "This will help you."

Obediently Anna drank, though the tea tasted terrible. Benjamin leaned against her and looked at her with wide eyes.

"Now you have some color on your face again," Henry said. "You will feel better by the minute."

"I'm sorry," she said. "The delicious soup..."

"We'll eat it soon. Do you want to stay here for a while? We'll leave Bennie with you. He kept saying, "I want to stay with Anna."

"Henry, I don't know what happened."

"Let it be for now, my girl. First of all, relax. We will investigate the question at a later date."

Benjamin stayed with her and played quietly with the mouse. Now and then, he leaned over and looked into her eyes.

Later, Henry carried the nearly sleeping Benjamin upstairs to his room, and Martha escorted her upstairs.

"Should I wake you up tomorrow, or would you rather stay home?"

"Wake me up, please."

"Good night, my dear Anna," Martha said and kissed her on the forehead.

Chapter 10

Animal Communication

In the morning, sunlight filled the kitchen again. When Anna said good morning, Martha came over and hugged her.

Henry said, "Good morning, Anna. Your eyes are shining again. Unfortunately, your frog is not completely restored yet. Norbert and I have to try different options, but I'm convinced that we will find a good solution."

"Thank you, Henry. I'm very grateful to you." She looked around. "Where is Bennie?"

"In the garden. I asked Miriam to bring him in," Martha said, "but it's been a while. Can you please get them?"

Anna heard Miriam's voice as she walked into the garden. Miriam and Benjamin faced each other.

Her little brother's back was stiff, and Miriam's face looked tight.

"Come, Benjamin," Miriam said. "How many times do I have to tell you? Come with me into the house. Come, hold my hand."

Benjamin stood with his legs apart, his arms at his sides, and his hands clenched into fists.

"Come on now!"

Silence. Anna saw Miriam keep her eyes fixed on Benjamin. The little boy did not move. Something happened between the two of them that Anna could not see, but she felt an intense tension.

"Bennie," she said softly.

He took a deep breath and turned to take her hand. Together, they went to the kitchen. Miriam followed slowly.

"Will you come to me today or should we come to you?" Julius asked on the way to her classroom. "We have not talked for ages."

Anna laughed. "But we are talking. Right now, for example."

"Not really."

"I know what you mean. I'm coming to you this afternoon."

Today they would get their first lesson in animal communication. Anna looked forward to it.

Wendelin Roth stood in front of the class and said, “When Professor Armstrong walks in, you get up and say, ‘Good morning, Professor Armstrong,’ and once Professor Armstrong has said good morning, you sit down again, okay?”

Some students laughed softly. The door opened, and a young man in a gray robe walked in. The class had learned their lesson and remained seated.

The instructor was medium height and slim. He had short brown hair that curled up, and he smiled shyly as he came in. He carried a cage covered with a cloth and set it down gently on the desk before standing next to Wendelin Roth in front of the glass wall.

“This is Tim Brown,” Wendelin Roth said.

Tim Brown nodded to them. He had friendly eyes.

Again, the door opened. This time a man in a black robe came in. The class jumped up.

“Good morning, Professor Armstrong.”

“Good morning, everybody,” he said, beckoning to them and leaning against the desk next to the cage.

His reddish-blond hair surrounded his head like the mane of a cozy and slightly disheveled lion. He had a short reddish-blond beard, and his voice sounded like a dark rumble.

Better not annoy this lion, Anna thought.

"You already know a part of my name. Now I'll tell you the other part—Frank.

"You're probably wondering what kind of animal is in this cage. Soon, you will let me know your guess. And please, be so kind to let me know your name before giving your answer. That way, I will learn your names during the year. So?"

The class was silent.

"You back there?"

"Juan Martinez. A small animal."

"Yes, certainly not a cow."

"And you back there to the right?"

"Lisa Bertram. A cat?"

"And you up here?"

"Karla Rossi. A chicken?"

"That would be a pretty taciturn chicken. Would anyone like to volunteer a guess?"

"Duncan McGregor. A rabbit."

"Simsalabim," Professor Armstrong said, pulling the cloth from the cage.

There actually was a rabbit.

Anna smiled at Duncan. "Well done," she whispered.

"There is no whispering or mumbling in my class. If someone has something to say, then they should say it clearly. Would you share what you said?"

"Well done."

"And how about your name?"

"Anna Cameron."

"And what, in your opinion, did he do well, Anna Cameron?"

"He knew that there was a rabbit in the cage."

"Do you think he guessed it well?"

"No. I mean, he knew it."

"And did you know it?"

"Duncan McGregor. Yes."

"Anna Cameron, I'm still interested in how you knew that he knew it?"

"I don't know. It just came to my mind."

"It just came to your mind," Professor Armstrong repeated and chuckled. He stroked his beard and said, "Now let's find out what else you know. What is the rabbit feeling right now? What does he want to do? You."

"Alexander Orlow. He wants to get out of the cage."

"Who else thinks this? Raise your hands."

Some students raised their hands.

"Okay, eleven of you. Let's see what happens."

He opened the door of the cage. The rabbit raised his head, sniffed briefly, and remained seated.

"Why doesn't the rabbit come out?"

"Cordula Müller. He is afraid to come out."

"Who shares her opinion? Raise your hands."

"There are fourteen of you this time."

Professor Armstrong lifted the rabbit out of the cage and set it on his arm. He stroked it and said softly, "Alright, buddy. You are safe."

Then he put it on the floor. The rabbit hobbled past the students and stopped near Melanie Pratt. She pulled her legs up into her chair.

"No great love of animals there," Professor Armstrong said.

The rabbit hopped to the glass wall and sat down in front of Tim Brown.

"What does the rabbit want now?"

"Julius Aquilas. He wants something to eat."

"Who of you shares Julius Aquila's opinion?"

More students raised their hands.

"Aha. Eighteen of you think that the rabbit wants to eat. What do you think, Tim Brown? Do you happen to have a carrot in your pocket?"

Tim Brown dug into a pocket of his gray robe, brought out a carrot, and handed it to the rabbit. The rabbit began to eat it.

The class clapped, and the rabbit dropped the carrot and ran back to Professor Armstrong.

"Applause is something that it is not used to. You scared it."

He picked the rabbit up and held it in his arms again, stroking it.

"Today you learned some important things about animal communication. First, animals are different than humans. They do not like applause, for example."

Professor Armstrong smiled.

"Second, when you turn your attention to animals, you can guess, suspect, or even know their feelings and intentions. At the beginning, there is still a lot of guessing, until one day you finally have a clue.

"You did pretty well today. With practice, guessing gradually turns into having clues. However, for most people, there's a long way to go from that to knowing the feelings and intentions of animals. Tomorrow we'll meet in the park."

He put the rabbit back in its cage, waved to them, and left the classroom. Wendelin Roth followed him.

When Tim Brown covered the cage with the cloth and carried it out, the minds in the classroom seethed.

"I felt from the beginning that the rabbit wanted out of the cage."

"Yes, but I suspected he was afraid to get out of the cage."

"Feel, guess, that's pretty nice. But I knew he was scared."

"Of course. If you were a rabbit, wouldn't you be scared if there were a bunch of people sitting around?"

"It was obvious to me from the beginning that he wanted to eat."

"Why didn't you say so?"

"Someone beat me to it."

"Nice excuse."

"That was a good lesson," Fiona said. "So interesting."

"That was dreary today," Melanie Pratt said. "Why should I care what a stupid rabbit feels?"

"You're right."

Her friends nodded and laughed.

As she walked out into the corridor, Anna saw that the four long-haired girls had stopped beside the entrance.

As she walked past them, Melanie Pratt leaned forward and said to her, "Just be careful that you don't have another fit when one of us talks to you."

Julius and Duncan had gone ahead of them and thankfully had not heard that. But Fiona, who was walking beside her, said, "Good gracious!", and squeezed her hand.

"Please don't tell the others about it. I don't want my parents to know. I don't want them to be sad on account of Miriam."

Chapter 11

The golden butterfly

Having tea together had always been a pleasure. During tea time, Anna's family told each other what they had experienced or wanted to do that day, and of course, they ate cakes or pies and drank tea. Most importantly, they felt comfortable.

Today there was fruit salad and nut slices, which Anna liked very much, but unlike previous tea times, this one made her feel bad.

Miriam came down the stairs in a dark green silk dress. In her hand, she held something that she showed Martha.

"My mother gave me this butterfly on my last birthday. I wore it as a pendant before I got the crystal. Isn't it beautiful?"

The butterfly was made of gold and set with rubies and emeralds.

"Yes, it's very beautiful. Henry, look."

Henry glanced at the butterfly. "Yes, quite nice."

Martha returned the golden butterfly to Miriam.

"Benjamin, don't you want to hold this beautiful butterfly?"

Miriam held the butterfly out to Benjamin, who looked at it with interest.

"Come, hold it in your hand."

Benjamin put his hands behind his back.

"May I watch your interesting work in the herb kitchen this afternoon again, Mrs. Cameron?" Miriam asked.

"Yes, gladly."

"And may I leave the butterfly here on the table until I go up tonight?"

"Of course."

If Miriam was with her mother in the herb kitchen, Anna could go to Julius's unnoticed. She had been afraid that Miriam would say that she wanted to come along just to annoy her.

"Anna, come to the workshop with me," Benjamin said. "I want to show you something."

She followed him and Henry into the workshop. There her little brother pulled her by the hand to his new magical toy, a large turtle. He sat down on it and rode around in the workshop, chuckling with pleasure.

"You'll be glad to hear that I have made good progress with the frog. He is already repaired to a large extent. Later, Norbert will come by so we can brainstorm how to revive your frog so that he has the same energy as before."

"That would be wonderful! Thank you."

For a while, she watched Benjamin romp about so happily on his turtle. Then she walked quickly across the meadow and over the bridge to the Aquilases' house.

Julius, Anna, Fiona, and Duncan walked down the stream, on the path Anna had walked with Julius so many times before.

"Do you remember how you fell into the stream?" Julius asked her.

"Oh, dear," Fiona said.

"Yes, she was six years old and could not yet swim."

"And then Julius jumped in to rescue me," Anna said to Fiona and Duncan. "The only problem was that he couldn't swim either."

"What happened?" Duncan asked.

"We clung to the roots of a willow," Julius said, "but we could not climb out. The current was too strong. Then, fortunately, Rex, the dog of my uncle Sextus, who was visiting, came running. He pulled us both out of the stream."

"Yes, first Julius and then me. Not chivalrous, the dog. He was supposed to get me out of the stream first, don't you think so?"

They laughed.

Duncan said: "Our father has a dog, a border collie called George. He is super smart. He finds sheep, even if they get lost in the blizzard, and drives them home.

"And if we want to shear sheep, our father just needs to look at George and whistle. Then George runs to bring exactly the sheep my father wants to shear."

Anna could hear the pride in Duncan's voice when he talked about his father and his dog.

"Do you know what's also remarkable?" Fiona said. "When George is home and my father gives him an order, George looks first at my mother for a moment. If she nods, he will follow the order."

"I'd like to meet that dog," Julius said.

"You will. You're going to visit us soon, right?"

By now they had arrived at Anna's and Julius's favorite spot at the brook, a bridge lined with weeping willows that dropped their branches into the water. They sat down on the bridge, dangling their legs and watching the water flow beneath them.

"And how is life at home with Miriam?" Julius asked.

"Miriam flatters them and is beastly with me, and my parents don't see it. And then I get beastly, and that's what they notice."

"That's terrible," Fiona said.

"At some point her mother has to come back from this concert tour. Then you'll be rid of her," Duncan said.

"Yes, she said 'at the latest for the Winter Celebration,'" Julius said. "And that's soon. You'll survive until then, Anna, though it's hard."

They got up and went back to the house.

"You're coming in, aren't you?" Julius asked. "Sophia wants to show you her new carpet pattern."

"That's what I intended, but suddenly I feel so restless. I think I should go home right now."

Julius looked at her searchingly. "Then you have to do that. Shall I accompany you?"

"No thanks. It's only a short way."

Anna hurried across the bridge and over the meadow, walking faster and faster, then went around the hedge and through the garden. She saw Henry and Martha standing by the aster beds under her window.

Miriam stood before them speaking. Benjamin cried.

"What's up?" Anna shouted before she even made it to them. "Why is Bennie crying?"

"Oh, Anna," Martha said. She had tears in her eyes. "He's still a little boy, and I should not grieve so much, but I never thought he would steal."

"He does not!" Anna exclaimed. "Bennie does not steal. He is the finest little boy in the world."

She knelt down and hugged him.

“With all due respect to your favorable opinion about Bennie,” Henry said. “Unfortunately, there is evidence of him stealing.”

“What happened?”

“Miriam wanted to go inside and saw Bennie burying her golden butterfly here. Look for yourself. The butterfly is full of soil. And you can still see soil on Bennie’s hands.”

Miriam. Always Miriam.

“Of course, there’s soil on his hands. He’s always digging in this garden bed.”

Anna stroked Benjamin.

“Did you ask him?”

“Of course. He admitted it.”

“Bennie, look at me,” Anna said. “Did you bury the butterfly here?”

“I buried nuts.”

“The butterfly? Did you bury the butterfly?”

“No butterfly. I buried nuts like the squirrels.”

“You heard it yourself. He buried nuts. He does that all the time. Why don’t you believe him?”

Now Anna also cried.

"Am I coming at an inopportune time?" Norbert asked.

They had been speaking so loudly that they had not heard him land.

"Norbert," Benjamin called.

Norbert picked him up and held him in his arms.

"Norbert," she said. "They say Bennie has stolen. But that's not true."

"Of course, that's not true," Norbert said. "Our Bennie does not steal."

"You have no idea what happened here," Henry said.

"I don't need to either."

"Miriam saw Bennie burying the butterfly."

"A butterfly, Bennie? I thought you liked the butterflies."

"A golden butterfly."

"Aha, and who says that?"

"I do," Miriam said.

There she stood in her dark green silk dress with her silver blond hair, which ranged lusciously and brilliantly to her hips.

"And who are you?"

"Miriam Andersson."

"Bennie, did you take the butterfly from Miriam Andersson and bury it here?"

"No butterfly. I buried nuts."

Miriam stomped her foot. "But I'm telling you!"

Anna stood next to Norbert and looked Miriam in the face. She saw Miriam's intense blue eyes on Norbert. They looked at each other for a while, the beautiful girl and the tall, thin man with his wild curls.

"And even if the emperor of China said that he had watched Bennie stealing, I would still believe my nephew."

With those words, Norbert turned around and walked into the house with Benjamin in his arms and Anna by his side.

The kitchen was lit by the glow of the light balls. The aromatic scent of tomato and cheese pastry wafted through the room. On the table sat cups and plates and bowls with a red maple leaves pattern.

How beautiful and cozy it looked, but was it still really cozy?

Norbert washed Benjamin's face and hands and dried them off. Then he sat his nephew on a chair. Meanwhile, Martha, Henry, and Miriam also came into the kitchen.

"What would you like to eat tonight, Bennie?"

"We have pastry," his brother said.

"Well, Bennie, what do you want to eat the most?" Norbert asked. "Nut cake?"

Benjamin nodded.

"You can have it. At least I hope so."

Norbert looked in the pantry.

"Here's the cake. And what do you want to drink?"

"In the evening, he always drinks chamomile tea," Henry said.

"Would you like to drink cocoa, Bennie? Warm, sweet cocoa?"

Benjamin nodded again. He had stopped crying, but he still sobbed now and then.

"Me too," Anna said.

Martha prepared the cocoa.

Anna was relieved when dinner was finally over. Norbert had carried Benjamin upstairs to put him to bed and tell him a story. Martha had come along.

Miriam played the organ, and Anna helped Henry in the kitchen. When they finished cleaning up, she quietly said goodnight and quickly went to her room.

What a day!

She turned off the light and sat on the edge of the bed. Would she even be able to sleep tonight?

Under her window, she heard two male voices. She crept through her room, leaning carefully out of the window and listening.

“I have been looking for you all over the house. Do I have to conclude from the fact that you are out here alone, that you are still angry with me?”

That was Henry’s voice.

“Yes. I had to get out of the house to calm down. I just cannot understand that you believe our Bennie less than this unknown girl,” Norbert said.

“But she saw him burying the golden butterfly.”

“So she claims.”

“Are you saying that she is lying? There is no apparent reason for her lying. Why should she do that?”

“I don’t know why either. All I know is that I trust Benjamin. He is an honest little boy.”

“Yes, he is, Norbert.”

“Then why did you not believe him?”

“I don’t know.” Henry’s voice sounded sad.

Norbert said, “Come on, let’s take a look at the frog.”

The voices moved away towards the workshop.

Chapter 12

Storytelling and Healing Arts

Anna's heart beat fast as she followed Eva Carpenter, Stefan Winter, and the study companion Tim Brown to the classroom where Storytelling was taught. She was glad that at least two students from her class had chosen the same elective and that she didn't have class all alone with the older students.

Tim Brown opened the door and walked into the classroom with them.

"Good morning, Professor Coppersmith," he said. "I brought you the new students—Eva Carpenter, Stefan Winter, and Anna Cameron."

"Good morning, Professor Coppersmith," the three first-years obediently said.

"Good morning," said the professor. "Come closer."

But they did not come closer. Instead, they looked around.

This room had a glass wall too, but the other walls were not just green like the walls of their classroom, instead, they looked like a flowering meadow. Anna had to smile. There weren't even any tables and chairs here. Instead, there were cozy armchairs all around.

And the professor himself, with his long gray hair and gray mustache, looked like a fairy-tale king, only without a crown.

"That's the kitten I almost knocked over the other day," said a tall student in an indigo school uniform who waved to Anna.

"Sit down, please," Professor Coppersmith said. "Here are a few armchairs for you. And who of you is Eva Carpenter?"

"I am," Eva said as quietly as she could, blushing.

"Let's continue from where we left off. Someone is walking across a meadow looking for something he or she has lost. Something important. Let the scene arise in your imagination, and if you think you have it clearly enough in mind, please raise your hand."

A student in a yellow school uniform told a story about the walk across the meadow, then a student in blue, and another student in green.

“Which description did you like the most? The first, second, or third? Please give hand signals. So, the second one. Why? Let’s ask the kitten.”

He pointed to Anna.

Anna stared at him, startled. “I don’t know, Professor Coppersmith.”

“Well, let’s see. Let’s start with the first story. Did you see the grasses and flowers with your inner eyes when the story was told?”

She nodded.

“And did you also see the sky and the clouds? And what about the birds? Did you hear birds? Yes?

“Now think of the third story. Did you also see the grasses and flowers in your imagination? And the sky and the clouds? And did you hear the birds? Was there something that you did not experience in the first story?”

“Yes, the wind. I felt the wind.”

“Good, and now the second story that most of you liked the most. Did you also see the grasses and flowers, the sky and the clouds? Heard the birds? And felt the wind?"

She nodded.

"Was there something that was missing in the other stories?"

"Yes, the man who walked across the meadow was worried."

"Thank you, kitten," the professor said.

"My name is Anna Cameron."

"Strange. I already suspected that. If you're not Eva Carpenter, and obviously not Stefan Winter, then you have to be Anna Cameron. A confident kitten."

The class chuckled. Anna had just started to get angry when she saw Professor Coppersmith's eyes. Big brown eyes that winked friendly. She breathed in relief.

The lessons went by quickly, and she went back to her classroom with Eva Carpenter and Stefan Winter.

"Sit down, please," Wendelin Roth said. "The professor will be here soon."

Today the class was not as obedient as usual. The students stood around and told their friends and table neighbors about their lessons in their electives.

Wendelin Roth clapped his hands. "Hey, sit down and listen."

Slowly, the class became quiet.

"The professor who will be teaching you Healing Arts is Matilda Kennedy."

He had barely finished speaking when the door opened. In came a very slim woman with a long black braid hanging down her back. Her black eyes glided quickly over the students.

The now experienced students stayed seated because this woman wore a gray robe and not a black one. With almost inaudible steps, she walked to Wendelin Roth and stood next to him.

"This is Amitola," Wendelin Roth said.

The student companion stared at the students with a serious expression. The students stared back. Only Amitola? No family name?

"It means 'rainbow,'" Wendelin Roth said.

When the door opened again, the class sprang up, and rightly so. This had to be the professor because she wore a black robe. Behind her came a small dog.

"Good morning, Professor Kennedy."

"Good morning," she said in a pleasant voice.

"You can sit down. I would like to introduce Kira, my animal companion, to you. She is a Cavalier King Charles Spaniel."

Kira paced back and forth, lifting her head and sniffing.

"Oh, how sweet," and "cute," and "pretty," the students commented.

"Sit down, Kira."

The little dog obediently sat next to the desk.

As impressed as Anna was with the study companion Amitola, she was disappointed with Professor Kennedy.

Anna thought that the professor, with her curly brown and gray hair reaching down to her shoulders, looked insignificant. She was neither ugly nor beautiful and had no interesting or exciting features, as one would expect from a professor of the famous Quentin Academy of Magical Arts and Sciences.

However, she had one beautiful aspect, her big gray eyes. And her little dog.

"You all have the gift of healing," Professor Kennedy began. "For some of you, the gift is weak, and for others it is strong. Also, the different families have their preferences on how to heal. What kinds of healing do you know?"

That sounded quite reasonable.

The rest of the class seemed to think so too because the answers came quickly.

"Healing with herbs."

"Healing with laying on of hands."

"Healing with crystals."

"Distant healing."

"Healing with energies."

"Healing with flower essences."

"Healing with sound."

"I'm impressed by how much you already know," Professor Kennedy said. "Do you know, then, what universal energy underlies all these healing arts?"

Silence. What kind of universal energy? Anna mused. What could that be? Martha could have answered the question with ease. Great-grandmother Marie could too.

“Think about it. Take your time.”

No answer came.

“You really don’t know? Then I want to tell you. This universal energy is love.”

Anna heard Julius snorting softly next to her. She had just been thinking that the professor was quite sensible, but now? How much she would have preferred to be in Storytelling!

“Is there anyone among you who is just not feeling well?” the professor asked.

Anna had not been feeling well day in, day out since Miriam moved in with her family, but she was careful not to say so. If she did, then the long-haired girls would scoff even more about her.

“No one? You in the second row on the left. Please come forward.”

John Adams approached hesitantly.

“What’s your name?”

“John Adams.”

“Wendelin Roth, please be so kind as to move my chair from the desk forward so that John Adams can sit. Thank you. Please sit down, John Adams.”

He sat down carefully, as if the chair could suddenly develop teeth and bite him.

"Now I ask you to envision a scale from zero to ten. In this case, the number zero means that you are not feeling well at all, and the number ten means that you feel great. On this scale from zero to ten, how do you feel?"

"Uh, I don't know."

"What's the first number, on a scale of zero to ten, that comes to your mind when you think about this question?"

"Five?"

"Good. So it is five. Please close your eyes, John Adams. The class will now send you friendly thoughts and good energies. What I ask you to do," Professor Kennedy said to the class, "is to think 'I love you. I love you.' with John Adams in mind. Continue doing so until I tell you to stop."

After about two minutes, Professor Kennedy said, "Thank you all. John Adams, you can open your eyes again. How do you feel?"

"Not that bad."

"On a scale from zero to ten—how are you feeling?"

"Seven, Professor Kennedy."

"Thank you, John Adams. Please sit down in your seat. Who wants to try this next?"

Many students wanted to try it out now. Among them were Carla Rossi, who went from four to six, Alexander Orlow, who raised his good energies from five to eight, and Lisa Bertram, who moved from five to seven.

But when Fiona sat in the chair and the class sent her good energies, everything changed. Fiona turned pale and frowned.

"Stop," the professor said. "Everyone stop. Fiona McGregor, how are you feeling?"

"Not so good, Professor Kennedy."

"On a scale from zero to ten—how did you feel when you started?"

"Six."

"And on a scale from zero to ten, how are you feeling now?"

"Two."

Professor Kennedy looked at the students in turn. "I wonder why," she said softly.

"I am very sorry, Fiona McGregor. I did not expect such a thing. Please sit back in your seat and close your eyes for a moment."

Professor Kennedy looked intensely at Fiona. The class was quiet. No one whispered or murmured. Anna did not dare to hold Fiona's hand in order not to get in the way of the suddenly very serious-looking professor. But to her relief, she saw Fiona smile after a few minutes. Her face became rosy again.

"Kira will be sitting at your feet for the rest of the lessons," the professors said.

The lesson continued, but they did not enjoy it as much as before.

Chapter 13

The little oak

Anna deeply inhaled the scent of damp earth as she walked into the greenhouse with Julius, Fiona, and Duncan. A forest of tree-children surrounded her. Coniferous trees and deciduous trees stood there side by side in their flowerpots on the transparent shelves in front of the glass walls.

"Anna," Fiona cried, "look, your tree."

Her tree, the little red oak, lay on the ground. Its flowerpot was broken, the soil was scattered, and the oak leaves had drooped.

She looked at her miserable little tree and did not move. What else?

"That's outrageous," said Julius. "What a cowardly act. If I find out who did it, he will regret it.

After all, the tree couldn't have jumped off the shelf on its own."

He looked around angrily. John Adams, Lisa Bertram, and Alexander Orlow, who stood next to Anna and her friends, waiting to take their own trees, stooped to pick up the pieces. Edith Kalmar, standing behind Alexander Orlow, became even paler than usual and retreated into the background.

Poor Edith. She couldn't stand conflicts. Neither could Anna. Not anymore.

"Don't worry, Anna. We'll help your tree get back on its feet," Julius said.

Help the tree back on its feet. She was so tense that she had to laugh out loud. Her classmates looked at her. They probably thought she was daft. Nevertheless, she could not stop laughing.

"Stop it, Anna," Julius said.

He looked at her so severely from under his black, thick eyebrows that she stopped laughing immediately. Now she was closer to weeping but weeping she had better under control. She'd had a lot of practice at controlling her tears recently.

"At least your tree still has its roots," Duncan said. "I'll get a new flowerpot. There must be one lying around here."

Julius lifted her tree carefully. “Where can I water the tree?” he asked Tim Brown, who had come closer.

“Oh, the poor tree,” the student companion said. “Come on, I’ll show you where the water is.”

Meanwhile, Duncan had come back with a new flower pot. Fiona took the pot and followed Tim Brown as well.

“I’ll get the right soil.”

When Professor Angelo came in, Anna, like the other students, sat in one of the chairs in the semi-circle with her tree in her hands. Like the others, she jumped up and said, “Good morning, Professor Angelo,” then sat back down.

Professor Angelo looked at her students and their trees kindly. Then she startled.

“What happened to your tree, Anna Cameron? It looks miserable.”

Professor Angelo came quickly to her, bent over her tree and clapped her hands. As she parted her hands, tiny energy stars rose from her palms. Professor Angelo gently put her hands around the small oak tree. The energies floating from her hands vanished, seeming to be absorbed by the small tree, which slowly lifted its leaves.

"Ah," Anna said, and the whole class also seemed to say "Ah."

"Thank you, Professor Angelo," she said. "I am very grateful to you."

"You are welcome. We have to do what we can for our tree companions. After all, they are our friends.

"But back to class," the professor said, without wasting time. "Eva Carpenter, please sit down on this chair here in the middle so that everyone can see your tree, the dogwood. And you, students of Class One, look at the tree with open or closed eyes, whichever you prefer. Keep your mind calm and feel the tree."

Anna would have liked to keep her mind calm, preferably from morning to evening, but these days she did not succeed.

After a while, Professor Angelo asked, "Well, who wants to share their impressions with us?"

Several students raised their hands.

"Stefan Winter?"

"It feels good."

"And you, Cordula Müller?"

“Something nice.”

“What’s your impression, Duncan McGregor?”

“Something beautiful.”

“You have already recognized some aspects,” Professor Angelo said. “The dogwood reminds us to see beauty in all things. The tree has this property, and people who are in tune with that energy express it. Eva Carpenter, you can sit back with the others.”

The small professor walked back and forth and looked at them with her dark eyes.

“You, Julius Aquilas, please sit down on this chair here in the center. You others, what kind of tree does he have?”

This time, many students came forward.

“Yes, Carla Rossi?”

“A pine.”

“And you, Lisa Bertram?”

“A juniper.”

“And you, Juan Martinez?”

“A cedar.”

“Right, a cedar. Now find out what the characteristics of a cedar are.”

Minutes of silence passed. Again, the students struggled to keep their minds calm and to discover what the cedar was all about.

"Now let's hear what you found out. Who wants to share their opinion with us? Alexander Orlow?"

"Definitely something great, Professor Angelo."

"Who else? Konstantin Richter?"

"Pride."

"Carla Rossi?"

"Stubbornness."

"Fiona McGregor?"

"I think it's courage, Professor Angelo."

"Correct. Courage." Professor Angelo smiled. "Good progress today. Please put your trees back on the shelves."

On the way out, Carla Rossi approached Anna menacingly. What was Carla Rossi up to? Probably nothing good. As Carla Rossi stood almost a head taller than her, it was best to stop as a precaution.

"Get lost, Rossi," Julius said, "and save your poisonous remarks."

He must have looked formidable because Carla Rossi turned around without a word and walked on.

On the flight home, Anna tried as best she could to close her ears against Miriam's remarks. But she nevertheless heard Miriam say, "I bet you did that on purpose."

Anna's curiosity was aroused. "Did what?"

"Well, throw down your tree when we left the greenhouse last time. You seem willing to do anything to get back in the spotlight."

Anna was speechless with amazement. Then she shook her head and said, "Can you think of nothing other than who's in the spotlight or not?"

At tea, there was a surprise. Just as Martha poured another cup of tea for Henry, they heard a carpet land. Energetic steps approached.

"Am I welcome to tea time?" Augusta Cameron asked.

"You are welcome at all times, sister dear," Henry said, and he stood up to hug her.

Martha also hugged her and Benjamin called, "Augusta, Augusta."

Augusta Cameron, a tall woman with short blond hair, kissed Benjamin and Anna.

"Come sit next to me," Henry said. "We missed you."

"Thought it was time to visit you," Augusta said. "Heard that Ingrid Andersson's daughter is living with you right now."

She went to Miriam and reached out her strong hand to shake Miriam's delicate hand.

"I'm Augusta Cameron," she said, sitting next to Miriam instead of her brother.

"I'm Miriam Andersson. I'm very pleased to meet you, Mrs. Cameron."

"Heard your mother sing in Boston," Augusta said in her harsh voice, "a remarkable experience."

"My mother would be honored if she knew you had found her concert remarkable," Miriam said sweetly. "I'll tell her about it. Thank you for your good opinion."

"Never mind," said Augusta, blushing. "Is your mother still on tour in Sweden?"

Anna couldn't believe it. Augusta blushed? This strong, self-confident woman blushed as Miriam sweet-talked her?

Henry put a plate of fruitcake in front of Augusta, and Martha poured her a cup of tea. Augusta didn't seem to see any of it. She was completely captivated by her conversation with Miriam and did not even notice when her family left the room after a while.

When Anna went upstairs in the evening, Miriam stood in the hallway at her door.

"Are you waiting for me?"

"Yes, I am." Miriam came up close to her and said, "Don't think you'll always win. Soon the tide will turn."

Anna lay awake for a long time that night. It was quiet in the house, and everyone else seemed to be sleeping well. She would have liked to be comforted by someone. But by whom?

Chapter 14

Animal Festival

It was Saturday, a mild October day. The sun shone. Little white clouds moved slowly across the sky. The day of the Animal Festival, which Anna had been impatiently waiting for, had finally arrived.

Everywhere in the world, the Animal Festival was celebrated. The families honored the animals that lived and had lived with them as well as the animals in the great outdoors.

For the first-year students at academies throughout the world, this day was of particular importance because today they would meet their animal companions.

Like many other families, the Camerons also prepared to fly to the Quentin Academy of Magical Arts and Sciences. Martha and Henry sat on the family carpet. Benjamin snuggled up against Henry while Miriam sat down next to Martha. Anna settled down on Augusta's carpet between Augusta and Norbert. These carpets had been woven and programmed by Augusta, so it would be a quiet flight.

Hector and Katinka stood expectantly beside them.

"You are waiting at home," Martha said. "We can't take you with us because there are already enough animals at school today. But you should be happy. We will bring two animal children home."

As they approached the academy, Anna saw carpets laden with families of first-year students flying in from all directions. Families with small cats and dogs on board were also heading for the landing site.

What a throng in the air! And what a crowd on the big square behind the academy!

Finally, the last carpets landed and were stowed away. The crowd of colorfully dressed families formed a large circle on the landing site. Between them stood the professors in black and the study companions in gray robes.

The director, Professor Roberts, stood in the middle of the square, her black cat next to her.

"Pinkus," she said to him, "please sit down there next to Professor Armstrong until we're done with the ceremony."

Obediently, Pinkus went to Professor Armstrong and sat down next to him.

Despite the black robe she wore, the director seemed to glow. Anna could not decide if it was the sun shining on her long blond hair or the gleam in her green eyes that spread that sheen around the director.

"My word," Norbert said softly next to Anna, just like when he had seen the director on the first day. He seemed to like her.

Professor Roberts welcomed the families with children, the families with animals, and the animals themselves.

Then she said, "Guests with the animal children, please bring the animals to me in the center."

They brought the animals to her, put them on the ground, and went back into the crowd of families.

"Students of Class One," the director said, "please step forward and make a loose circle around the animals. Leave two steps between each of you. We want to make the choice easier for the animal children."

The students found their places in the circle after a lot of back and forth, and then Professor Roberts said in a loud voice that echoed across the square, "Class One of the Quentin Academy of Magical Arts and Sciences, in an instant, you will send out a mental call as if you are calling in your mind. With this call, you will attract your future animal companion.

"Please close your eyes now and send out love and joy together with your call, and the right little dog or cat will come to you. After the call, you can open your eyes again. Call your animal companion —now!"

Like the others, Anna called her animal companion with enthusiasm. *Whether you are a dog or a cat, I will love you.*

Then she opened her eyes and saw the animal children turning and looking around. Some raised their heads and sniffed the air. Then a few small dogs and cats came to the students. After that, more and more started to move.

Was the cute little dog with her extra-large ears approaching her? Was that her animal companion? She did not dare to move so as not to affect the animal. Yes, the little female dog sat down in front of her and looked at her shyly.

"Do you want to come to me? Do you really want to live with me? Oh, thank you! You're such a wonderful little dog. May I pick you up?"

She felt the little dog in her arms, so warm and soft. "I love you," she whispered.

"Anna, Anna," Julius called. "Look at my great dog! I'll put him down on the ground. Look, doesn't he look really defiant and brave? He is an Akita. I named him Amicus."

Julius picked him up again.

"Yes, you are right," she said. "He looks really confident. That's so cute in a little dog. Look, here's my dog."

"She's great," he said. "Her big ears are especially cute. She looks like a German shepherd hybrid. Her face is so pretty and so is the dark border around her eyes—just great. I've never seen such a dog. Actually, she looks more like a wolf. No, like a coyote. In any case, she is terrific."

Edith scurried past them.

"Edith, stop," Anna said. "Let's see your cat."

Edith blushed. What was the matter with her lately? Whatever was going on, Edith stopped and showed them her little cat.

"She is a Russian longhair cat," she said. "She has silver-gray fur. Isn't she beautiful? And my mother says that these cats are particularly gentle and friendly. I already know what her name is: Tinka."

"What a beautiful little cat," Anna said.

"Yes, isn't she? But I was wondering …"

"Wondering what?" Julius said.

"I'm wondering …" Edith's voice became gradually lower, "I'm wondering if I deserve such a very beautiful cat."

"Of course, you deserve her. She is the right cat for you," Julius said.

Edith snuggled her face against her cat's fur. Were those tears Edith was hiding?

"Anna! Julius!"

Fiona and Duncan approached with their treasures in their arms.

"This is a Maine coon tomcat," Fiona said excitedly. "He's getting big. My uncle Patrick has one. He is very smart and independent—the tomcat, I mean, my uncle too, actually—and very lovable. His name is Tommy. I'm so happy with him."

"Understandably," Julius said. "Such a handsome cat. And you, Duncan, what kind of black-and-white fur bundle do you have under your arm?"

"Fur bundle, are you kidding me? This is a female border collie. They are super. Do you remember what I told you about George, my father's dog? She is such a very special dog too. Her name is Ellie."

The long-haired girls went past. "Look, the carrot heads seem to have found normal animals," Carla Rossi said.

"Yes, maybe there are not enough pet freaks," Melanie Pratt said.

"Oh, she is gorgeous! Look, that woman there."

Carla Rossi pointed at a tall woman with creamy-white skin, coral-colored lips, grass-green eyes, and copper-colored curls that surrounded her head. The long-haired girls and other people turned to the woman as she approached.

Yes, Anna also thought the woman was extremely beautiful. Fiona ran up to her.

"Mama," she called, "look, what great animals we have."

All the students except for Miriam had found their

animal companions.

“Where’s my dog?” she wailed with her piercing voice. “Has anyone seen my little dog?”

She started to cry.

Professor Roberts came up to her and asked, “What happened? Did you lose your dog?”

“No, he did not come to me to begin with. I wanted the Dalmatian puppy. Someone must have snatched him from me. Instead, this stupid cat who doesn’t belong to me is sitting here.”

The director, who had smiled so friendly before, frowned. “This little cat here,” she said, lifting her gently, “is a domestic shorthair. These cats have lovable characteristics. They are active, curious, playful, and also calm. You should be happy to have such a wonderful animal companion.”

“But I don’t want her,” Miriam howled. “Everyone has great animals. Even Anna has a pretty little dog! Why can’t I have one?”

More and more people moved closer to listen.

“My own pet companion is a tomcat,” the director said. “He’s the best animal companion I could wish for. But what do you mean when you say that someone snatched your dog from you? Did the Dalmatian puppy originally approach you or someone else?"

"He came in my direction—there he is." Miriam pointed accusingly at Eva Carpenter, who carried a small Dalmatian in her arms.

"Give him to me."

Miriam jumped towards Eva, but a strong arm held her back.

"Take it easy," Norbert said.

"What happened with your dog, Eva Carpenter?" Professor Roberts asked. "Did he approach you or Miriam?"

"He approached me, Professor Roberts. Miriam was not around at all. Why? Did I do something wrong?" Eva Carpenter asked. Her lips trembled, and she wrapped her arms even tighter around the little Dalmatian.

"No, everything is in order."

"If the girl doesn't want our dear little cat, we'll take her home," a man said, reaching for the cat, which still sat on Professor Robert's arm.

"The cat has chosen," the director said seriously. "We can't ignore that."

"If I may make a suggestion, Professor Roberts," Henry said, who had come up with many others. "With Miriam Andersson living with us right now, I would like to suggest that this little cat will be received by our family on behalf of Miriam Andersson. Although it seems unlikely from today's perspective, it cannot be excluded that Miriam Andersson might change her mind over time."

Professor Roberts nodded.

Then Henry turned to the man who had brought the little cat.

"I am Henry Cameron. I would be glad if you accept my suggestion. I can assure you that your cat will be happy with us. She will be loved and cared for along with our own animals. If Miriam Andersson will not have a change of heart, the little cat will stay with us as a member of our family."

The man looked at Henry inquiringly and then nodded. "Agreed," he said, shaking Henry's hand.

Professor Roberts handed the cat to Henry, who held her gently in his arms, and then turned to face Miriam, who was still crying and sobbing.

"Miriam Andersson," she said. "Without love, you walk a thorny path."

With these words, she turned and walked into the park, where refreshments were available for all, including the small animals.

The families were just beginning to settle into the armchairs in the park and admire their new family members, taking turns holding them in their arms, when shouts and shrieks came from the square in front of the academy.

“A dragon! A real dragon!”

A stream of people spilled around the school building to the forecourt, speaking lively and loud.

“I thought dragons were long gone.”

“Dragons are magical beings. They can even speak.”

“I’ll believe that only when I hear them speak.”

“Hopefully he will not spit fire.”

“Dragons are just mythical creatures. They don’t really exist.”

But there actually was a dragon.

The crowd in front of the castle surged back and forth. The newcomers wanted to see what was going on and pushed forward, and those who stood in front did not want to be pushed too close to the dragon and pushed back.

"Make room for the director," Norbert shouted.

The crowd parted. With quick steps, Professor Roberts approached the dragon, but Julius was faster. With Amicus in his arms, he ran past her and called, "Sable Tooth! What are you doing here?"

The crowd fell silent, looking and listening.

"You call, I come."

"Oh, Sable Tooth, my dear friend," Julius said. "I'm so grateful you've answered my call. I am always happy to see you. To honor the truth, I called an animal friend, but not you, dear Sable Tooth. My call was for a young animal to become my animal companion. And he came. Here he is. His name is Amicus."

He raised Amicus up, who growled and showed his teeth.

"Brave Amicus is. Sable Tooth your friend no longer is?"

"Oh, Sable Tooth!"

Julius lifted an arm, and the dragon lowered his head. Julius stroked his neck.

"You are my friend forever and ever. But you can't stay here. My parents' house is too small for you, and this school is not built for dragons.

"You belong in the grand castle of my grandparents and the vast land there. My family there, and all the other people in the castle and in the village, need you. You want to protect them, right?"

"Protect I want."

The dragon moved his wings. The crowd backed away. Only the director remained standing next to Julius.

"Stop! Sable Tooth, wait! I want to introduce you to the director of my school."

"Professor Roberts, this is Sable Tooth, our dragon friend who has lived with my family for generations."

Dragon and director bowed to each other. The dragon unfolded his wings again.

"Wait, do not fly away yet. Here come my parents."

Lucius and Sophia Aquilas approached the dragon.

"What a joy to see you again, Sable Tooth," Sophia Aquilas said, stroking his neck.

"Your visit is an honor to us," Lucius Aquilas said, bowing low.

"The honor mine is," Sable Tooth said and bowed, too.

Julius said, "These are my friends Duncan McGregor and Fiona McGregor."

They, too, bowed to the dragon, and Sable Tooth bowed his head in greeting.

"Twins a strong alliance is," the dragon said.

"And this is my friend Anna Cameron, of whom I've told you so many times, with her brother Benjamin Cameron."

Anna extended her hand to the dragon, who lowered his head so that she could stroke him.

Benjamin hid his face on her shoulder, but then he looked at the dragon nevertheless. Sable Tooth bent his neck even lower, and Benjamin stroked his huge head.

"Bold Benjamin Cameron is," the dragon said. "Small and great at the same time."

The dragon unfolded his wings again. The bystanders moved further back.

"If in danger, Sable Tooth you call, Julius?"

“Yes, on my honor.”

With a loud beating of his wings, the dragon rose higher and higher into the blue sky, turned south, and disappeared on the horizon.

The people in the square in front of the school remained quiet for a while.

Finally, a woman said, “It is amazing that I was allowed to experience this! One day, I’ll be telling my grandchildren this story.”

Chapter 15

Of small and big animals

"This woman is right," Augusta said. "I also didn't think that I would ever see a dragon. Thought they were extinct."

The two carpets flew home side by side.

"How fortunate we were to experience this wonderful event," Martha said. She held the little cat in her arms. "And on top of everything, we also have these cute little animals. What a wonderful day."

Benjamin snuggled up to Martha and stroked the kitten. "Kitten, kitten, kitten," he sang.

"Did Julius ever tell you about the dragon?" Norbert asked.

"Oh, yes, often," Anna said. "During the summer holidays, he flies with his parents to his Aquilas grandparents' castle where Sable Tooth lives. When he comes back, Julius tells me what he and Sable Tooth did on vacation."

"What they did on vacation?" Norbert asked. "What can you do with a dragon?"

"Mrs. Aquilas told me that Sable Tooth has taken good care of Julius since he was a little boy," Anna said.

"I can't imagine for the life of me," Henry said, "how such a great dragon could watch over a lively little boy like Julius was."

Anna smiled. "Sable Tooth lay down in the grass and let Julius climb all over him."

Everyone laughed at this idea, except for Miriam, who frowned and didn't say a word.

"And nowadays?" Norbert asked. "What are they doing now?"

"During the last summer break, they went to the river or into the forest. When it rained heavily, Sable Tooth was allowed to enter the great hall. Sable Tooth does not mind the rain, but his grandparents wanted Julius to stay dry.

"There, Sable Tooth and Julius talked and told stories. Sable Tooth could listen to stories from morning to night."

"My word," Norbert said, "a dragon who likes to listen to stories."

Anna stroked the little dog in her arms.

"Henry, how do people bring the right number of the right animals to the Animal Festival?" she asked.

"I think the Council of the Wise has something to do with it."

"And who are the Council of the Wise?"

"All I know is that they live in seclusion and wear white robes," Martha said. "Do you know more about them?" she asked the others.

"They are kind of wise teachers with extraordinary skills," Augusta said.

"And how do the animals know who to go to?" Anna asked.

"I think the animals and the kids are a good energy match," Augusta said. "The animals seem to know where to go. Anyway, I'm very happy with my Molly."

Anna smiled as she thought about how her stern and energetic Aunt Augusta spoiled her little Pomeranian with treats.

"Julius immediately named his dog Amicus. Fiona and Duncan also knew what to call their animals. I'm the only one who can't come up with a name."

"Maybe it will help you," Martha said, "to look her in the eyes."

"Look at me," Anna said, smiling at her dog.

The dog raised her head and looked at Anna with her amber eyes.

"Kaylee," Anna said after a while. "Her name is Kaylee. Bennie, my little dog's name is Kaylee."

"Kaylee, Kaylee, Kaylee," Benjamin sang.

"What a beautiful name," Martha said. "Let me follow my own advice and look this kitten in the eye."

For the first time on the flight home, Miriam said something. "Lola," she said. "Her name is Lola."

Hector and Katinka were waiting for them when they landed behind the house. Hector wagged enthusiastically when he saw Kaylee and Lola. Katinka meowed and rubbed her head against Martha's legs.

"What can I serve to celebrate the day?" Henry asked. "Coffee, tea, or wine?"

"Thanks, but I have to go home right away," Augusta said. "Molly is waiting for me."

"And Toby is waiting for me," Norbert said.

"I can believe that Molly is waiting," Henry said. "But Toby is the most patient dog I know. You just want to get back to your work."

"You know me too well," Norbert said. "Yes, I'm running an experiment that I have to take care of. But I'll be back tomorrow. I would like to compare my research results with yours. And besides, we have to take care of the frog again."

"Martha and Henry, is it okay with you if I skip the tea today?" Anna asked. "I can't wait to show Kaylee our garden and the house."

"I come with you," Benjamin said.

Hector was already there, and Katinka and Kaylee were waiting beside him. Nobody needed to ask Lola. The little cat followed Katinka on her own.

Anna hesitated. Should she ask Miriam if she wanted to come along? She avoided Miriam whenever she could, but Miriam had at least given the little cat a name. She gave herself a jerk and asked, "Miriam, would you like to come along to show Lola her new home?"

"What have I got to do with Lola? Do what you want."

Anna had intended to introduce Kaylee and Lola to their new home, but it was the adult animals, Hector and Katinka, who led the animal children, Benjamin, and her around the house, past the dog and cat doors, through the garden and beyond the hedge to all the places that were important for animals.

From that evening, she no longer slept alone in her room, for Kaylee slept by her bed in a comfortable dog bed that Martha had prepared.

That night, she could barely fall asleep because she kept looking at Kaylee. Her little dog seemed to feel the same way, because whenever she leaned down, Kaylee looked up at her.

Chapter 16

Quiet times

In the following weeks, the first-year students learned more about plant communication. Through practice, they learned to calm their minds so that they could better interpret the energies of trees. In addition, they learned more about the main characteristics of their own tree companions and the tree companions of their fellow students.

Fiona's beech meant tolerance, Edith's blue spruce peace, and Miriam's magnolia had something to do with difficult choices.

Anna was surprised to learn that the main characteristic of her own tree, the red oak, was to honor her own inner wisdom and power.

"Professor Angelo," she asked one day, "what is the main characteristic of the linden tree?"

"To enjoy the peace and snugness of home."

The class also made some progress in animal communication. Professor Armstrong often took them to the forest, where they learned to interpret the characteristics and intentions of squirrels, deer, blue tits, and mice.

Anna practiced animal communication in a very different way with her friends at the Aquilases', where they taught "come" and "sit" and "stay" and "give paw" to their dog companions.

The four friends had also wanted to practice these commands with Fiona's Maine Coon, Tommy, but he just looked at them, remained sitting beside Fiona, or sniffed around them. However, he did come when they called him.

"What kind of strange sounds does Amicus make?" Anna asked one day. "It sounds like he's always talking."

Julius laughed sheepishly. "Yes, he likes to babble."

"I think that's cute," Fiona said.

"Yes, I think so too," Duncan said. "Amicus seems to add his commentary everywhere."

"Lucius says that I have to train Amicus well. He says that he is a powerful, protective, and independent dog with a strong will. Lucius thinks that Amicus will only become a good animal companion if he reliably submits to the necessary discipline. And if he does that, he will be terrific. I hope I can do it."

"You can do it," Anna said. "Anyone who is friends with Sable Tooth will be able to train Amicus."

The autumn weeks passed fairly peacefully. Miriam still spent her afternoons with Martha in the herbal kitchen. Bennie played in Henry's workshop or came with her and Kaylee, and sometimes Lola, to the Aquilases'.

At the academy, the long-haired girls, with the exception of Miriam, proved difficult in a new way. Now they wanted to make friends with Julius.

"Man, is that disgusting," Julius said. "Whenever I turn around, one of them grins at me. That's worse than before."

Anna was beginning to think she might survive well through the arrival of winter vacation until the call came.

Chapter 17

Preparations for the celebration

As soon as she saw Benjamin waiting at the landing site behind the house, Anna knew that something out of the ordinary had happened. He waved to her.

"The crystal has talked," he said.

Martha came out of the house and said, "I'm glad you are back. Please come to the house immediately. Miriam, your mother called a few minutes ago, and she'll call back soon."

Miriam ran past Martha into the house.

"The crystal has talked," Benjamin said again. "I also want to talk to the crystal."

"Well, I don't know if the crystal wants to talk to you," Anna said, "but you'll certainly be allowed to listen."

Benjamin grabbed her hand and hopped beside her.

The comcrystal stood on a low transparent pillar in the living room. Martha and Miriam had already sat on the chairs in front of it. She sat down next to Martha, Benjamin in her lap.

The comcrystal was, as always, transparent with many facets. But just as Henry came in, a loud "bing, bing, bing, bing, bing" sounded, and the crystal began to glow and flicker. The image of a woman appeared, bright in the white-gray light.

"Mama," Miriam said.

"My warmest greetings to all of you," the still flickering Ingrid Andersson said. "And especially to you, my beloved daughter Miriam."

"Oh, Mama," Miriam said again. "How much I missed you."

Really? Anna was surprised.

"Greetings," Martha said.

"Good day," Henry said.

"Hi," Anna said.

Benjamin seemed to have lost his voice. He snuggled closer to her.

"I would like to take this opportunity to thank you, my dear Martha, and you, Mr. Cameron, wholeheartedly for the hospitality you extend to Miriam. Knowing that she is in the best of hands with you lit up my lonely dark days here in Sweden."

No wonder Miriam spoke so stiltedly. She had gotten that from her mother.

"Hearing about your lonely and dark days in Sweden—do I take it that the concert tour was not that successful?" Henry asked.

"Oh, it has been a complete success. The concert halls are filled to the last seat. The people here are at my feet. I am showered with invitations and presents."

The image of Ingrid Andersson flickered more violently, and her voice could only be partially heard, something about gifts for Miriam and the Camerons. Then the contact broke off. The crystal returned to its normal state.

"We often have storms over the Atlantic this time of year," Henry said. "There are frequent interruptions in communication."

"Mama," Miriam said again. "I want to hear my Mama."

She started to sob.

Again they heard the “bing, bing, bing, bing, bing.” The crystal flickered. Ingrid Andersson’s image reappeared in its white-gray light.

“It seems to me that in between the connection was interrupted,” Ingrid Andersson’s voice said. “I want to apologize for that. The last thing I want to do is waste your precious time.”

“Mrs. Andersson,” Henry said, “if you have something to say, please say it now and quick.”

“Uh,” Ingrid Andersson said, “so what I meant to say is that of course I originally wanted to come back for the Winter Celebration. But now something has come up...“

Her image and voice again disappeared.

“But what?” Miriam howled. “Why does she say ‘but’?”

Anna wondered that too. Again they heard the “bing, bing, bing, bing, bing,” and the flickering Ingrid Andersson appeared. She said something about a really fantastic offer. The connection became more and more patchy, went and came back.

Then Ingrid Andersson said something about a special concert evening at the Winter Celebration in Rome. Then the connection broke off and did not come back.

"What?" Miriam screamed. "Mama is not coming back for the Winter Celebration?"

Martha and Henry tried to comfort her, but Miriam went crying upstairs to her room.

Anna heard the heavy slamming of the door. Poor Miriam! Her mother would not come to the Winter Celebration, and she herself avoided Miriam wherever she could and did not want her friendship.

She was much happier with Julius, Fiona, and Duncan, and of course with Bennie, Martha, Henry, Norbert, Augusta, her grandparents, Katinka, Hector, Lola, and Kaylee.

Why couldn't she like Miriam better? What a bad person she was that she couldn't like her! Now she, too, ran sobbing into her room.

Weeping, she lay on her bed until she heard a scratching at the door. She let Kaylee in and took her in her arms. After a while, she calmed down. She forgave herself for her shortcoming and decided to have a new start with Miriam. From now on, she wanted to be particularly friendly and patient with Miriam.

When they flew home the next afternoon, she asked Miriam, "Would you like to go to the Aquilases' with me this afternoon, or would you rather play and sing to me what you have learned in music lessons?"

"Save your pity," Miriam said, looking at her intensely. Her blue eyes seemed to grow bigger and bigger, and her voice sounded hollow. "Today you can still laugh, but the laughter will soon pass away."

"No," Anna called.

She wrapped her arms around herself and closed her eyes. She was cold, so cold.

This year, Anna was especially looking forward to the Winter Celebration. The day before the actual Winter Celebration with the families, they had a day off from school to help with the preparations. Anna thought the preparations were actually the best part.

And then came the Winter Celebration itself and then the Winter Celebration at the academy, where students of different classes put on shows for parents, siblings, and of course for the school community itself. Then the winter holidays started.

Norbert and Augusta arrived early in the morning to help with the preparations. In addition to delicacies for humans and animals, they brought along the cute little Molly and Norbert's elegant male collie, Toby.

While people discussed how best to rearrange the furniture and prepare the house for the guests, the animals sniffed, wagged, or meowed and retired to the warm kitchen.

The large glass doors between the living room and the rarely used social room were pushed apart so that both rooms now opened to create a particularly large room.

Henry and Norbert activated three additional energy fireplaces to keep the house warm enough even in a blizzard. Martha, Anna, and Augusta adjusted armchairs and tables so that the room was comfortable for quite a large crowd of guests.

Benjamin jumped around enthusiastically. He wanted to help but got in everyone's way. Miriam was not visible.

So far everything had gone well, but then a question about the walls arose.

"Leave it to me," Norbert said, projecting a mountainous snowy landscape across the walls with rugged rocks, a waterfall with icicles, and snow-covered slopes.

"I'm already getting cold watching," Augusta said.

"How about my idea?" Henry said.

A moment later, the walls were covered with a winter forest with small and large snow-covered fir trees and deer eating at the haystacks.

"Still cold," Augusta said. "Martha and Anna, I think we should check out the food supplies while the boys enjoy their winter landscapes here."

The pantry next to the kitchen had different temperature ranges, from below freezing to room temperature.

On the shelves, were cakes and tarts, vegetable pies and stews, jams, breads, biscuits, croissants, butter, cream, cheese, pizzas, vegetable casseroles, chocolate in various shapes, and baskets of nuts, vegetables, and fruits.

"Guess your parents and mine will bring something to eat, too," Augusta said. "Have to make room on these shelves."

"We can do that easily," Martha said. "We can take the nuts, jams, and fruit somewhere else. I can make some more room in my herbal kitchen. Fortunately, I can seal the shelves in my herbal kitchen at will, so the food will not be affected by the various herbal scents."

When tea time came, everyone in the house was exhausted, thirsty, and very cheerful. Everyone except for Miriam, who wasn't with the others.

"I'll look for Miriam," Martha said. "With all the back and forth, I did not notice that she wasn't here."

Anna had also completely forgotten Miriam for a time.

"Thought that you, Miriam Andersson, would sit next to me," Augusta said as Miriam came in with Martha. "We can talk a bit about music. Do you sing yourself?"

A harmless subject. Surely Miriam would not cry when she talked about her music lessons.

Little Lola had made herself comfortable on Martha's lap. The other animals had also flocked to the family. While the family drank tea and ate nut pastries and cheese biscuits, Miriam talked about her singing instructions.

They were almost finished with tea, and still Miriam hadn't howled or complained about her mother. Maybe they were in luck.

"Must confess," Augusta said, "that I'm looking forward to meeting your mother tomorrow."

It was bound to happen eventually.

"My mother," Miriam said, "my mother is not coming tomorrow. Her voice and extraordinary art has caused a great stir. She has been invited to sing tomorrow at the Winter Celebration in a famous concert in Rome."

She must have been working on that answer for a long time.

"Rome in Italy? Noteworthy," Augusta said. "Only too bad for us here."

"Yes, too bad," Miriam said, hanging her head.

Miriam looked like a brave heroine. Did she always act? Most of the time, probably. Only recently, when her mother called, had she been real.

Amazingly, they once again heard a "bing, bing, bing, bing, bing." They hurried into the living room. Ahead of all of them was Miriam, who called, "Mama, Mama."

But it was the grandparents Margaret and John Summerfield.

"Grete, Grete," Benjamin called and, "Johnnie, Johnnie."

"Good evening, dear Bennie," John said. "And good evening, to you all, our loved ones. May we come tonight? The storm here on the Atlantic Coast is getting stronger. Who knows how strong it will be tomorrow."

"Oh, please come," Martha said.

"Yes, please," Henry said. "You would make us very happy."

"Good flight!" they called before the picture went out.

That evening, Anna had trouble falling asleep again. This time, not because she was sad or scared, but because she was happy.

Kaylee slept by her bed. Henry, Martha, Bennie, and she were surrounded by their family. Augusta and Norbert were here along with the dear grandparents Summerfield, and tomorrow the grandparents Cameron would also come.

For the first time in a long time, she felt safe. Everything would be fine.

Chapter 18

The Winter Celebration

Suddenly, Anna woke up. It was not her frog that had woken her like usual. He sat still only half-repaired on one of the shelves in Henry's workshop. Even her Kaylee, who slept next to her bed, was very quiet.

It was—she heard it again—it was Bennie happily talking to himself, walking down the hall. Why was Bennie up here at this time in the morning? And then she realized why. It was Winter Celebration, and he was going to see the grandparents Summerfield.

She jumped out of bed and ran down the hall with Kaylee, after Benjamin, who was just opening the door to Margaret's and John's room.

"Grete, Grete," Benjamin called, climbing into his grandmother's lap.

He laughed at her and stroked her face as if he couldn't believe that Margaret was really here.

John and Margaret sat in the small armchairs in front of the table by the east window and drank tea. That was always the first thing they did in the morning—prepared Earl Gray tea, drank, and talked while looking out the window.

They had pulled colorful silk robes over their pajamas. They were just as uncombed and unwashed as their grandchildren and just as happy.

Margaret, with her short white curls and friendly smile, radiated such well-being that everybody wanted to sit down beside her at the table.

John, on the other hand, with his gray hair, short gray beard, and light green eyes under thick black eyebrows could scare you until you saw his occasional wink.

Lili, Margaret's blue-eyed white cat, jumped onto Margaret's lap next to Benjamin while Hermes, John's English foxhound, sighed softly and moved closer to John's chair.

Anna sat down on the floral carpet at their feet.

"I can't tell you how happy I am that you're here," she said.

"And we're glad to be with you," Margaret said. "We're also curious about your houseguest who did not show up last night."

"Miriam Andersson," she said. "Yes, well…you will meet her."

"Do I sense a lack of enthusiasm there?" John asked.

She was always surprised how quickly her grandparents Summerfield got to the heart of the matter, like carrier pigeons reaching their destination. But she didn't want to talk about Miriam, so she held up Kaylee and said, "Here's my Kaylee. Isn't she wonderful?"

Kaylee was greeted, caressed, and admired by Anna's grandparents, and sniffed by Lili and Hermes.

"Wait a minute," Margaret said. "We have something for your little dog."

She rummaged in her suitcase and then handed Kaylee a stuffed rabbit with long ears almost as tall as Kaylee.

"It's soft and durable at the same time," John said. "She can chew on it as much as she likes, and it will not rip or tear through."

He chuckled. Then the grandparents admired Benjamin. They praised him for how much he had grown and how well he could speak. Her grandparents also complimented Anna on her elective Storytelling.

“It’s the best subject you can choose,” Margaret said with a smile.

“An assessment that will not surprise anyone who knows that you have that special gift yourself, my dear,” John said and kissed her hand.

Someone knocked on the door.

“I just wanted to warn you,” Norbert said through the closed door. “Breakfast is ready, and my parents have just arrived.”

“Thanks for the warning, Norbert,” John said. “If we’re lucky, we’ll not be scolded if we hurry now.”

Margaret laughed softly.

“Bennie, run quickly into your room,” Anna said. “Go into the fresh chamber and dress as fast as you can. Mama has probably already put your clothes out. I’ll hurry too.”

Anna met her grandparents Cameron in the kitchen. They had just greeted Benjamin, who wore his tunic backwards.

“Come along to the hall,” Kurt Cameron said, “so we can fix your tunic away from the public eye.”

Benjamin hopped cheerfully after him.

“Anna,” Elise Cameron said. “Come, let me hug you. You are already such a big girl that you go to the Quentin Academy. Excellent! Which scientific subject did you choose as an elective?”

Elise, whose special gift was Mineral Communication and whose husband excelled in Magical Mathematics, did not even consider that Anna might have chosen an art subject.

At that moment, Augusta came in, followed closely by Miriam.

Anna heaved a sigh of relief. With Augusta and Miriam nearby, they would certainly talk about music and not about her elective.

“Breakfast is ready,” Henry said. “Please come to the living room to eat.”

Kurt Cameron, who went ahead of everyone, stopped when he saw the walls. Two showed a winter forest and two a snowy mountain landscape.

“Certainly, thanks to your cooperation, Henry and Norbert?”

His sons stood next to him and looked at him expectantly. The three men were so similar—all tall and slim with dark eyes—except that Kurt's curls were gray instead of brown.

"Beautiful and atmospheric pictures," Kurt said. "But could we possibly have a cozier environment?"

The walls became white.

"John, you are the master of art here. What do you suggest to us?"

"A quick fix so that the pancakes and croissants don't get cold. Just a sunny yellow."

The walls turned a sunny yellow.

Nearly everyone sat down, only Kurt remained standing.

"I thank you, my dear children, on behalf of the whole the family, for the beautiful Winter Celebration you have prepared for us. We are pleased with it and happy to be here with you."

He looked at each of them in turn with a smile.

"Today is the darkest day of the year," he continued, putting his hands on his heart. "On the return of the light!"

The others also put their hands on their hearts and repeated, "On the return of the light!"

Anna was lucky enough to sit between Margaret and Martha. Benjamin could not decide where he wanted to be. Sometimes he sat on Margaret's lap, sometimes on Elise's, and sometimes on Martha's.

Then he went to Kurt, to John, to Henry, to Norbert, then outside to the big dogs he admired, especially Norbert's collie Toby.

Now Benjamin had returned to her. She had already eaten a warm chocolate croissant and was taking a second one when Benjamin said, "I also want to drink coffee."

Since her coffee was enriched with so much milk and sugar, she let him drink from her cup. Nevertheless, Benjamin grimaced and said, "Coffee is bitter."

She looked around, as all ate and drank so contentedly, conversed, and occasionally laughed. If only she could hold on to this moment. She wanted to always be as happy as she was now.

But even the most beautiful Winter Celebration breakfast came to an end. They cleaned up and dressed warmly for a walk with the dogs. They walked across the large meadow to the creek and along the stream. The dogs galloped around them, only Molly walked close to Augusta.

Benjamin, who had already run around all morning, was alternately carried by Henry and Norbert.

When they came back, Norbert, Henry, Kurt, John, and Benjamin discussed how they wanted to decorate the walls for the afternoon and evening. They agreed on fir trees without snow but with many wax candles, as one used to have them in earlier times. The imagery festively illuminated the room from all sides with its golden light.

The tables were set again, this time with nut cakes, creamy cakes, pastries of all kinds, chocolate, tea, and coffee. No sooner had they finished than they heard carpets landing and happy voices as the Aquilases and McGregors came in with their dogs and cats.

Anna had to smile. It was almost as loud as at the academy landing site when the students landed and everyone had a lot to tell each other.

But after tea, it was quiet as Margaret, at the request of the family, sat down at the sound-light organ and began to tell a story. She told them about departure and adventure, about salvation and homecoming.

The sounds and light patterns of the sound-light organ accompanied her voice. Margaret enchanted her audience with her narrative art. They suffered and hoped with the hero and breathed a sigh of relief when everything ended well.

Time passed, but Anna barely noticed. To be able to tell a story in such a wonderful way was such a gift! When the story came to an end, it took her a while to find herself at home at the Winter Celebration. The others seemed to have similar experiences.

“I have never heard such a beautiful story,” said Miriam. “Thank you, Mrs. Summerfield.”

“Do you know where Bennie is?” Martha asked Anna.

“No. Maybe with Elise?”

He was not there.

“Henry, do you know where Bennie is?”

“No, I haven’t seen him for a while. I thought he was with you or our parents.”

More and more relatives and friends asked about Benjamin, and finally, they started looking for him.

Martha, Elise, Margaret and Augusta went outside searching for Benjamin in the herb kitchen and in Henry's workshop.

Anna, Julius, Fiona and Duncan ran through the house, peering into every room, and calling Benjamin. Why did not he answer? He was such a friendly little boy. He would certainly answer if they called him. Finally, they opened cupboards and chests and looked under beds, constantly calling his name. All in vain.

"Where can he be?" she said. "Surely not in the pantry?" She opened the door to the pantry and looked around there, too, but Benjamin was not there.

"As long as it takes, we'll definitely find Bennie," Julius said, pulling his thick black eyebrows together. "He's probably in the meadow with the dogs."

Anna's heart beat fast. She was struggling to catch her breath. Bennie could not just have disappeared, or could he?

"Julius is right. We will find Bennie." Fiona put her arm around her.

"Absolutely," Duncan said. "After all, Bennie cannot disappear into thin air. He has to be around."

"Yes, let's go outside," Julius said. "Maybe the others have already found him by now."

Family members and friends who had turned up with dogs searched for Benjamin outside. They walked around the house and through the garden with their dogs, finally, they checked behind the hedge and in different directions across the meadow.

They came back one after another, asking hopefully, "Is Bennie back?"

But Benjamin was and remained missing.

Chapter 19

The search

Anna saw lightning and heard thunder in the distance. A thunderstorm moved closer.

"Oh, Bennie," Martha said and cried. "He is so afraid of thunderstorms."

Henry hugged her.

Anna looked around. Relatives and friends looked worried and depressed.

"We have to organize our search better," Kurt said. "Haste is required."

He projected a map onto a kitchen wall that showed the Cameron and Aquilas houses and the land around them, along with the forest and creek.

"We will form two teams," Kurt said. "The dog team will include those who have dogs. They will search certain areas on the ground with the dogs, especially along the stream.

"Those who belong to the carpet team will fly close to the ground with headlamps turned on, also in certain areas."

Then Kurt turned to his eldest son.

"Henry, will you please fly Julius Aquinas, Fiona McGregor, and Duncan McGregor to the Aquilas family's home so they can help and comfort Benjamin if he shows up there?"

Fiona hugged Anna, sobbing. Duncan patted her on the shoulder, and Julius said, "One of us will find him. Sure." He squeezed her hand so hard that it hurt.

"Take it easy, my girl," Henry said softly, hugging her. "Even if the situation looks grim now—when so many of us are looking for Bennie, we will find him."

They left the house.

"Anna and Miriam Andersson," Kurt continued, "you will stay here in the house for the same reason."

"No," Miriam wailed, "I don't want to stay here and wait. I can't deal with this. I want to help find dear Benjamin."

"I think we all know what to do," Kurt said. "We just have to..."

"No, no, no," Miriam howled.

Kurt looked at her in surprise.

"All right," Augusta said. "Take her along on my carpet. Molly can't join the dog team anyway. Is afraid of thunderstorms."

As the teams organized themselves, Anna went into the living room and sat down in one of the comfortable armchairs. The fir trees with the candles still lit the room festively, but it no longer felt festive. Was it really only earlier today when she had wanted to hold a happy moment of this Winter Celebration in memory forever?

And now Bennie was missing, and nobody knew where he had gone. Nobody knew why or how, and all joy had passed.

Norbert came into the living room. The fir trees disappeared, and the walls turned white.

"Oh, Anna," he said when he saw her.

He hugged her, and suddenly she could cry. It was better to cry in Norbert's arms than to sit there alone, rigid with terror and suffering.

“Can you make the walls cozy again?” she asked after a while.

Hills of fir forests appeared under a pearl gray sky with a hint of dawn on the horizon.

“Better?” Norbert asked.

She nodded. He went to the comcrystal and entered coordinates. An image of Gabor Kalmar appeared in the white-gray light. The picture flickered because of the thunderstorm, but she could still see Gabor Kalmar smiling happily when he saw Norbert.

“What an unexpected..,” he said. Then he must have seen Norbert’s expression because he asked, “What...how...help?”

“Benjamin,” Norbert said, clearing his throat. “Benjamin has disappeared, my little nephew. I want to ask... “

The image flickered even harder than before, but she could still hear Gabor Kalmar saying, “Come immediately...”

Then Julianna Kalmar’s flickering image appeared.

“Me too...” she heard the slightly distorted voice of Julianna Kalmar. “Come...own carpet.”

The picture went out. Norbert sighed and set new coordinates.

In the white-gray light, she saw the flickering image of Professor Roberts. The director was festively dressed and smiled.

"Please forgive the disturbance," Norbert said. "Could you maybe contact Wendelin Roth? As far as I know he lives in Oakville. Benjamin has disappeared, my little nephew, the brother of Anna Cameron. Maybe Wendelin Roth can help search."

He swallowed.

She wondered how much the director could understand with the bad communication signal. But Professor Roberts seemed to understand well enough, because she heard the director say, "Wendelin... Oakville...come too..."

The connection broke off. For a moment, Norbert remained standing there. Then he put his arm around her shoulders and walked with her back into the kitchen, which was teeming with humans and animals.

"Can you add four helpers to the search teams?" he asked his father.

Now the dog team was on the way—Norbert and his collie Toby, John and his English foxhound Hermes, Kurt and his setter Einstein, Sophia Aquilas and her dachshund Emma, Wendelin Roth and his Russell terrier Sam, and Angus McGregor and his famous George—each of them searched a particular grid in the meadow, brook, or forest.

The carpet crew had also taken off. Professor Roberts, Wendelin Roth, and Julianne and Gabor Kalmar had been greeted briefly, but gratefully. Now the Kalmars and Professor Roberts flew with Martha, Henry, Margaret, Elise, Lucius Aquilas, Augusta, and Miriam in an assigned grid across the country in search of Benjamin.

Henry had joined the carpet team because Hector couldn't be persuaded to leave the site behind the house.

Where was Bennie? What happened? Now, alone in the kitchen, apart from the cats and small dogs playing or sleeping there, Anna felt her fear for Bennie grow stronger.

What could she do? Sit around? She could see after Hector, who was still out in the rain and thunderstorm.

Hector sat with his head hanging behind the house on the family landing site. He raised his head as she approached and looked at her with his golden eyes. She crouched down next to the golden retriever. *What do you want to tell me, Hector?*

She had to find out. After all, she'd had lessons in animal communication. Although her heart beat anxiously because of Bennie, she tried to calm her mind, to feel less anxious, to look at Hector, and to listen.

It was important to Hector to stay here. She could feel that. She could also feel how loyal and reliable he was. Important, reliable, loyal. What did that say to her?

And suddenly she understood. Hector remained loyally where he had last seen and sniffed Bennie. Here on the carpet landing site. This was the last place Bennie had been before being abducted on a carpet.

"Hector! You good friend!"

She hugged him and cried and kissed him on the head.

"You are the only one who saw that. You're the only one who knows what happened. And in your own way, you're telling us what has happened, staying here in the rain and thunderstorm."

The others searched in vain because they couldn't imagine that someone could intentionally harm a child. It was unimaginable that someone would kidnap Bennie! Bennie, whom they all loved. All of them, except for one person.

"Hector," she said, "I'm going to the house now because I have to do some things before I leave with you. Come along. Then we'll go, you and I, to find Bennie."

Hector followed her into the kitchen. There she filled the feeding bowls for the dogs and cats and gave them fresh water in various bowls. Hector did not eat, but he did drink.

She ran to her room and sat on the edge of the bed. She knew that Bennie had been kidnapped on a carpet, but where was he now?

How could she find out? She imagined her little oak. How had she learned about her oak? Be calm, feel it. Impressions came to mind. They had often practiced that in class with trees and animals. She could do that with Bennie, too.

Bennie? Where are you, Bennie?

After a while, something cold came to her mind, something white. Snow. He was in the snow. He was in the mountains.

How could she share this insight with her parents and grandparents? Should she wait until they came back? But with Bennie in the snow, she couldn't wait. She had to find him as soon as possible. What should she do?

Again, she thought of her red oak and its main characteristic.

"Honoring the wisdom and power within," Professor Angelo had said.

She had to do that now. Trust and act on her inner wisdom.

She put on her winter school uniform, which were her warmest clothes. After pulling over the hooded cloak, she stuffed her gloves into the cloak's pockets. She put on her padded boots and wrapped the long cherry-red scarf around her neck. Then she ran to the kitchen.

"Katinka," she said, "I have to leave and give you the responsibility for the animals here. Look after them and keep them from doing anything stupid. Hector and I will be back as soon as we can."

The black and white cat looked at her and meowed.

Anna went out with Hector into the stormy evening. They hurried across the meadow, over the bridge into the grove, through the garden in front of the Aquilases' house, and into the living room where Julius, Fiona, and Duncan sat by the energy fireplace, talking softly.

"Anna!" Julius jumped up. "What's the matter?

"I know where Bennie is," she said. "He's in the snow somewhere near your house, Fiona and Duncan. We have to hurry. It's snowing."

"How do you know that?" Duncan asked.

But Julius said, "Not now, Duncan. What should we do, Anna?"

"Get dressed as warmly as I am and take your scarves. Come to the kitchen as fast as you can. We'll talk during the flight."

In a few minutes, the others returned, and they followed Julius silently to the carpets. He pulled the school carpet out of the shelf and unrolled it. Quickly they sat on it, and Hector lay down next to Anna.

Then Julius switched on the force field and said,

"To the Quentin Academy of Magical Arts and Sciences."

The carpet took off, and now she had time to tell them what she had experienced.

Gusts of wind shook the fully laden carpet and hailstorms pelted the force field, but the carpet flew steadily on to the Quentin Academy.

"Good Hector," Julius said as he stroked the dog after he had heard Anna's story. "You are a loyal and honorable friend."

"Do you think that maybe Miriam kidnapped Benjamin?" Duncan asked.

"I don't know how it all relates," she said. "Miriam seemed to be there the whole time. But no matter who it was, Bennie was kidnapped with a carpet. I got an impression of Bennie in the snow, so we have to look for him there. We have to trust our inner wisdom, right?"

"But what if our carpet is no longer at school?" Fiona asked.

"If! If! If!" Julius said, banging his fist on the carpet with each *if*. "Then we'll just come up with something else."

The carpet labeled *McGregor Duncan, McGregor Fiona*, was still in its compartment. They stowed the Aquilas carpet and took off to the west with the McGregor carpet, into the mountains.

Anna suddenly felt cold and weak. She closed her eyes.

"Anna, you're so pale," she heard Fiona say.

"Lie down for a moment," Julius said. "Even if it's tight here. Maybe you can sleep a lap. We are traveling for almost an hour. For now, everything is fine here."

She wanted to say, "I can't sleep now," but somehow, she couldn't say that. The next thing she heard was Fiona, who said, "Wake up, Anna. We've arrived."

She saw through the force field how heavily it was snowing. She heard the wind howling around the force field and shuddered. Her little brother was out there.

"Before I turn off the force field," Julius said, "pull on your hoods and tie the scarves tightly around you."

The force field dissolved. Suddenly it was dark and cold.

"Oh, Bennie," she said.

Julius put his hand on her shoulder.

"We'll find him," he said. "We have the wise and brave Hector with us. We'll bring Bennie home."

They got up. The wind drove snow in their faces. Hector shook himself.

"Oh, my goodness," Fiona said, "if we leave the carpet here, the snow will bury it in the blink of an eye, and we'll never find it again."

"Don't worry," Duncan said. "The carpet will definitely come with us."

He shook the snow off the carpet and pressed the names on the side. The carpet rolled up, and Duncan took it under his arm.

Anna saw Hector running around them in small circles, sniffing in the snow. Occasionally he stuck his head in the snow and blew in it. Then he must have found the track because suddenly he wagged, barked briefly, and trotted off.

"Stop, Hector, wait. We have to stay with you."

The golden retriever plodded on.

"Hector, sit," Anna said.

Hesitating, he sat down and trembled with impatience. She wrapped one end of her scarf around his neck and knotted it there, holding the other end like a leash.

Hector trotted ahead again, sniffing and occasionally barking. They followed him, sliding and stumbling.

"Wait," Duncan shouted. "I slipped and fell and lost the carpet."

"Anna, stay here and keep hold of Hector," Julius said. "Fiona and I will help Duncan search for the carpet."

Fiona and Julius had gone only a few steps and already she felt abandoned in this cold, windy, dark world full of snowstorms. Hector was with her, the faithful, reliable Hector, but Bennie, on the other hand, was out there all alone. The little guy had to be so scared! She sobbed.

Shadows appeared next to her and condensed into the shapes of her friends.

"Anna, I'll knot your scarf with Hector on the other end around your right wrist," Julius said, "and my scarf around your left wrist. We'll make a chain with the scarves so we don't lose each other."

Onward they stumbled through the driving snow. Hector sniffed and lead them on and on and then stopped.

"Stop," Anna said, but Julius had already rammed her. She dropped to her knees.

"I'm sorry," he said. "What is Hector doing? Did he find Bennie?"

Hector stood in front of a dark hole and barked excitedly. Julius, Fiona, and Duncan knelt down beside her and stared into the dark hole.

"Bennie, Bennie," they called and then listened.

Hector barked.

"Hector, quiet!"

There was nothing to hear. Only the wind howled.

"Bennie, Bennie!"

Hector barked again, tail wagging.

"Shh."

There was something. A small voice said, "Anna?"

"Yes, Bennie, we are here with Hector," she called. "We'll get you out of there." She turned to climb down.

"Anna, let me do that," Julius said.

"No, I'll climb down there," Duncan said. "I know better about the crevices here."

"Absolutely out of the question," Julius said. "I'll get Bennie out of there. I know him as long as he lives. For me, that's a matter of honor."

"Matter of honor—rubbish!" Duncan's voice was rough with indignation.

"While you quarrel, Bennie freezes," cried Fiona.

"Come on, Duncan, be a good chum and help me with the scarves. Knot your scarf to mine and hold it tight. But do not pull on it until I tell you. I do not feel like plummeting into this icy abyss."

The storm blew snow so hard in Anna's face that she could only open her eyes for a few moments. So, she could barely make out how Julius gradually disappeared into the dark depth, and how Duncan lay down in the snow and bent his head over the edge of the crevice.

"Careful, Julius," he called. "Take your time!"

Hector barked excitedly, scratching in the snow.

"Hector, quiet!"

Fiona grabbed her arm. She felt Fiona tremble. Or was that her own trembling that she felt?

Then, despite the howling of the storm, she heard something rumbling.

“Julius, are you all right?” she called.

“Yes, it was just a piece of ice.”

“Must have been a big piece of ice,” Duncan said.

They listened again. Hector whimpered.

“I have him,” Julius called after a while. “I’ll tie now one end of the scarves around Bennie’s stomach and shoulders. Okay, now you can pull him up.”

They pulled the scarves up. Hector barked and wagged excitedly.

Benjamin shouted, “Anna, Anna.”

And then he was there with them. Benjamin clung to Anna. She and Fiona sobbed, and Duncan kept saying, “Now we have him. Now we have him.”

“Julius, where are you?” she called after a while.

“Blast it!” he called. “I’ve slipped lower. Everything is ice down here. I can’t reach the sheep. And I can’t get out of here by myself!”

“What sheep?” she asked.

“We can knot two scarves together and lower them. You can hold on to them while we pull you out," Duncan shouted down into the dark hole, letting down the knotted scarves.

Silence.

"It's not working," Julius called. "I can't reach the scarves. The wind is blowing them away from me. And if I bend over too far, I'm going to slip even deeper."

"Duncan, you can let me down with the two scarves," Anna said. "Then Julius can reach me and the scarves."

"Too heavy," Duncan said, "Fiona and I can't pull up both of you. However," he said, looking at Benjamin, "we could lower Bennie. The three of us can easily pull him and Julius up."

Bennie? Not Bennie! The poor little guy had just come up from that icy abyss. Still, how else could they save Julius?

"Bennie," Anna said, "we want to lower you down there for a moment so we can get Julius out. We'll pull you and Julius up right away. Can we do that?"

Benjamin leaned forward and looked back into the dark hole. He cried softly but nodded.

"Before we do that, put on my tunic," Anna said.

She took off her cloak and tunic and then quickly slipped back into her cloak. Fiona helped her dress Benjamin in the tunic and roll up the too-long sleeves.

"Are you ready?" she asked her little brother.

He nodded again. They cried themselves when they lowered Benjamin down and saw tears running down his face.

When they finally pulled up Benjamin and Julius, and they all lay in the driving snow on the cold but safe ground, they had to laugh. They laughed and laughed and wiped snow and tears from their eyes. Only Benjamin did not laugh. He clung silently to Anna.

Duncan was the first to remember what they had to do next. He put the carpet in the snow, leaned close over it, and pressed on the names *McGregor, Duncan; McGregor, Fiona*. The carpet rolled out.

"Come here quickly and sit down on the carpet."

They could barely see the carpet in the heavy snow and crowded close together to find space on it. Anna took Benjamin in her lap and called for Hector. The golden retriever stood next to the carpet, but he did not come. Julius leaned forward, wrapping both arms around the dog and lifting him up and above them.

"Now, Duncan," he roared.

The force field flickered. It was moderately bright. No more snow fell on them. Warm air poured in. Julius released Hector, and the dog fell on Julius and Duncan. Hector yelped. Duncan said, "Ouch." The carpet was overcrowded, but nobody could fall off. The force field protected them. They were safe.

"To the Quentin Academy of Magical Arts and Sciences," Duncan said.

The carpet took off, swaying in the gusts of wind, and flew steadily on.

Chapter 20

The return home

Anna held Benjamin in her arms and stroked him. He was shaking.

"Dear Bennie, good Bennie," she whispered to him.

"Benjamin, you have done well," Fiona said.

"Thank you, Bennie. You helped save me," Julius said. "Without you, we couldn't have made it. You were very brave."

"What is brave?" Benjamin asked.

"You allowed us to lower you down into that dark hole," Anna said, "even though you were afraid of it. That is called brave."

"I am brave?"

"Yes, you are brave," Julius said. "On my honor, you are brave."

"Absolutely," Duncan said.

"I am brave," Benjamin said, smiling.

The trembling stopped.

"And you, Hector, are a great friend," she said, stroking Hector, who with some back and forth, had managed to lie down next to her. "Thanks for helping us."

He looked at her and wagged his tail.

"You were all terrific," she said, looking at her friends one at a time. "Without your help, Bennie wouldn't be here with us now. Thank you."

"Sure," Duncan said.

"Anytime," Julius said.

"Of course," Fiona said.

They answered at the same time and then everybody laughed again.

"Ah," Anna said and sighed deeply. "How good to have friends."

"I am also a friend," Benjamin said.

"Sure, you're one of us," Julius said. "A brave boy like you."

When they came out of the mountains, it wasn't snowing anymore. It was raining. Anna saw the water running along the force field. The carpet swayed in the squalls but continued to fly towards Quentin Academy unwaveringly.

If only she could fly on with Bennie, Hector, and her friends in this small, warm world of the carpet. Nothing to do, nothing to decide. No questions, no dangers. Just being safe.

After a while, Fiona asked, "Julius, you said something about sheep earlier. What did you mean by that?"

"Well, when I had climbed and slipped down to Bennie, he was sitting on a small horizontal piece of rock between two sheep. They must have kept him warm because when I touched him, he was quite warm."

"Two sheep?" Fiona asked. "That's strange. Usually, only one sheep ever falls into a crevice. But two?"

"The poor sheep," Anna said. "Who will save them now?"

"My father and George will, when they get home," Duncan said. "They know how to go about it."

They changed from carpet to carpet at the Quentin Academy landing hall. The McGregors' carpet was returned to its compartment, and the Aquilases' carpet flew to the Aquilases' home where all the windows were brightly lit.

When they landed and got up from the carpet, the dachshund Emma ran to meet them, loudly barking. Amicus, Ellie and Tommy came running too. Even the dignified cat Cato strode toward them.

"They are here," Sophia Aquilas called. "Our children are back. Oh, wonder! They have found and brought Benjamin along!"

They were taken to the house and the living room in triumph, but then an avalanche of questions broke over them.

"Are you okay?"

"Are you hungry?"

"Are you thirsty?"

"Where have you been?"

"Why did you leave without telling us?"

"Thank the Creator and all the angels for your return!"

"What happened to Benjamin?"

And in between, Emma barked, Amicus grumbled, and Ellie yapped.

"My goodness, don't crush us," Fiona said.

"This is worse than the icy abyss," Julius said. Benjamin started to cry.

"Enough!" Deirdre McGregor said. "Give the children room to breathe."

As soon as Deirdre McGregor had said "enough," everything changed. What kind of magic did she use to bring about this change? The dogs no longer barked, grumbled, and yapped, but kept wagging their tails. And the people no longer asked questions but hugged the returned children, smiling or crying.

"But there's one thing I have to do, Deirdre," Lucius Aquilas said. "I have to call the Camerons right now. They should not be unhappy a minute longer."

He went to the comcrystal and pushed around on the input field, but no connection was made.

"Sophia, please help me. I'm so excited. I just cannot enter the correct coordinates."

Sophia helped him, and then the comcrystal began to glow and flicker. An image appeared. Anna's family gathered in front of the comcrystal, some with red eyes, others pale, but all full of expectation.

“They are here. Our children are back and brought Benjamin along. We’re all flying to you right now.”

Anna’s house was brightly lit, too. Deirdre McGregor went into the house ahead of them. Anna did not hear what she said, but when they came in, they were not overrun by an avalanche as they had been when they arrived at Julius’s house.

Someone took off their heavy cloaks and long scarves. Cups of warm cocoa were put into their hands. They were smiled at, caressed, hugged and kissed, but there was a certain calmness, a peaceful atmosphere.

Henry took Benjamin in his arms after he had already been lifted by nearly all family members.

“I am brave,” the little boy said proudly.

“I believe so.”

“He was really remarkably brave, Mr. Cameron,” Julius said, and so they began to tell their story.

After the adults had strengthened themselves with tea or hot soup while listening, and after discussing with each other the most interesting and courageous points of the adventure, Norbert stood up.

“I almost forgot to let the others know. They are still worried.”

He went to the comcrystal and told the Kalmars, Wendelin Roth, and Professor Roberts about the children’s happy return home, and everyone was relieved and grateful for the good news.

“The children are already closing their eyes. It’s about time they go to sleep, after all, it’s the school’s Winter Celebration tomorrow,” Martha said.

A loud “bing, bing, bing, bing, bing” sounded, and they hurried to the comcrystal.

“What’s going on so late?” Henry said, taking the call.

Gabor Kalmar’s face appeared in the gray-white light. He looked miserable and downright desperate. Edith stood behind him, hands clasped in front of her face, and sobbed. Julianna Kalmar stood in the background and cried.

“Come on, Edith,” Gabor Kalmar said, “take your hands off your face and tell everyone what you just told us. Tell them by the honor of the Kalmars.”

“I... I flew Benjamin to the McGregors’. But I didn’t know they weren’t home.” She wrung her hands.

The picture disappeared.

"Edith?"

"Not Edith!"

"Edith!"

Terrified silence.

Anna could not stand any more terror and horror today. Before the flood of questions and discussions came, she ran upstairs to her room without a word. She took off her clothes, left them on the floor, and ran to the sanitary chamber and then to her fresh chamber. Chamomile, warm, and gentle airflow.

She stayed there for a long time, not listening when someone knocked on the door of her room. She let the purifying and soothing energies wash over her until she found some relief.

Finally, she went back into her room, put on her nightgown, put her clothes in the refresher, and was about to go to bed when she realized someone was missing. Kaylee! How could she have simply forgotten her dear little Kaylee?

She walked barefoot through the house and down to the kitchen. Henry and Augusta leaned against the table talking. They looked serious. When the two siblings heard her coming, they turned to face her.

"Can I do something for you?" Henry asked with a smile.

"Have you seen Kaylee?"

"Think she's in an armchair in the living room near the door," Augusta said.

Kaylee slept on an armchair, curled up comfortably on her toy rabbit. Norbert stood close to the comcrystal, speaking softly and urgently to someone. She could not see or hear with whom.

Only when she turned around with the sleepy Kaylee and her rabbit in her arms did she see who Norbert spoke to—the director.

Chapter 21

The hearing

The sky was gray, and although the golden light balls spread a friendly light in the living room, the mood in the room reflected the grayness outside.

Anna looked at her family, who sat at the long breakfast table, which was richly covered with rolls, cereals, croissants, nut cake, butter, cheese, honey, and jam. They each drank coffee, tea, water, or juice, but ate little, for no one seemed to be hungry.

Benjamin took turns sitting on Martha's, Elise's, and Margaret's lap. Every now and then he said "Anna" and stroked her when he was near her.

Miriam sat next to Augusta, but for a change, she was silent. Kurt, Henry, Norbert, and John sat at the other end of the table talking softly. They looked worried.

The "bing, bing, bing, bing, bing" of the com-crystal rang out, startling everyone. The image of Wendelin Roth appeared. He looked serious and official.

"Professor Roberts, the director of the Quentin Academy of Magical Arts and Sciences, sends her greetings to the Cameron family through me, Wendelin Roth, and invites the following people to join us at the Quentin Academy in Conference Room One immediately upon completion of the Winter School Celebration: Martha Cameron, Henry Cameron, Norbert Cameron, Anna Cameron, and Miriam Andersson. Study companions will guide you to the Conference Room One. End of the announcement."

The image disappeared.

"What's going on?"

"What a surprise!"

"Things seem to be moving forward."

The family was unsettled, but then Augusta said in her measured way, "I'd like to come to the school festival, but I will take care of Benjamin and the animals."

Everyone calmed down a bit.

"We will help with cleaning up after the breakfast," Elise said. "Then we'll fly home."

"We'll help too," John said, "and then we'll fly home as well, but we'll be back soon."

After exchanging farewells, hugs, promises of visits, and consolations for Benjamin, who wanted to come to the Winter School Celebration, they finally flew to the Quentin Academy on Augusta's large family carpet. Anna heaved a sigh. It was the calm after the storm.

Or was it the calm before the storm?

She desperately wanted to have peace and quiet, but now was probably not the time. When she saw Julius on the landing site, she ran to him.

"Have you also been invited by the director?"

"Of course. All of us have. I wonder what's happening there."

She sat in her chair in the big auditorium like a cat on a hot tin roof although the classes had prepared beautiful events, plays, and choir singing, in which Miriam also participated. Professor Roberts thanked the students, wishing them pleasant holidays and saying goodbye to the families with a charming smile that showed her dimples.

As people poured out of the auditorium, Wendelin Roth and Tim Brown bowed to the Camerons, Aquilases, and McGregors, asking them to follow them to Conference Room One.

Anna watched as Norbert followed Miriam. It seemed as if Miriam wanted to disappear into the crowd, but Norbert stood in her way and said, "Right this way. Surely you don't want to get lost on the way to the conference room."

Conference Room One had a long row of comfortable chairs to the right of the door, in front of it sat a large desk with three armchairs behind it and a smaller row of armchairs to the left. Through the large windows on the right and behind the desk, Anna could see the park and the gray sky above.

A painting of colorful flowers, birds, and butterflies in a lush forest covered the whole left wall. She could barely look away from the beautiful and brilliant colors.

Wendelin Roth and Tim Brown led them to their seats in the long line of armchairs. Anna sat towards the right with Martha on her right and Henry on her left. Norbert sat on Henry's left, then Miriam, Angus McGregor and his family, and then the Aquilas family.

Wendelin Roth and Tim Brown positioned themselves to the left and right of the door.

When the director came in and went behind the desk, everyone rose.

"Thank you for coming here," Professor Roberts said. "Please be seated. Mr. Norbert Cameron, may I ask you to sit here next to me? Thank you. Wendelin Roth and Tim Brown, you are responsible for ensuring that nobody enters or leaves the room without my permission.

"Please let in the family who is waiting at the door."

Anna sighed when she saw who came in. It was Gabor Kalmar, Julianna Kalmar, and Edith, all looking pale and sad. The Kalmar parents were asked to sit in the chairs to the left of the desk, and Edith was led behind the desk to sit next to Norbert.

"Wendelin Roth, please close the door and bring the key to Mr. Norbert Cameron. Thank you."

The director looked at each of them in turn with a serious expression. Then she said, "The hearing is open. It will be recorded."

She tapped at the small crystal on her desk, and it started glowing and recording.

"For the sake of completeness, I would like to mention," continued Professor Roberts, "that I have also sent an invitation to Mrs. Ingrid Andersson who is at the Villa Lambordini in Rome, but unfortunately I have not received any answer so far.

"Now, Edith Kalmar, tell us what you did regarding Benjamin Cameron on the afternoon of the Winter Celebration. You may stay seated."

"I flew Benjamin Cameron to the McGregor family's house with Fiona and Duncan McGregor's carpet," Edith said in a shaky voice.

"Why did you do that?"

"I am not allowed to say that."

"Here you have to say everything according to the truth. So, why did you do that?"

"But I'll be punished if I say that."

"Your punishment for concealing the truth is far more serious than any punishment that you think you will have to suffer if you tell us the truth. Speak, Edith Kalmar."

"Miriam Andersson told me to do it."

Miriam jumped up.

"That's nonsense. She made that up only to wash herself clean. You don't just do what someone else says."

Angus McGregor nodded.

"Sit down, Miriam Andersson," the director said.

Miriam sat down angrily and looked intensely at Edith.

"Well, Edith Kalmar, please tell us what happened," Professor Roberts said.

"I...I don't know. No, Miriam didn't say anything. She has nothing to do with it."

"Allow me, Professor Roberts, to express my astonishment," Lucius Aquilas said. "A moment ago, Edith Kalmar said something totally different."

The families looked at each other in bewilderment and whispered together.

"I agree, Mr. Aquilas," Professor Roberts said. "Now is the time when I have to reveal two things to you with the approval of the Council of the Wise. First, I am a class A telepath. This is the strongest class. Second, Mr. Norbert Cameron is a class A thought controller, also the strongest class.

"We both have been through a long and rigorous education at the School of the Council of the Wise at various times throughout our childhoods, which is why we can resist the temptation to use our gift for selfish reasons.

"The gifts of telepathy and thought control are a blessing to the community, but they can become a curse if they are not properly controlled by the individual who has the gift, much like an uncontrolled wildfire."

The Aquilas, Kalmar, and McGregor families had already experienced a lot of excitement in the last few days, but now they were thunderstruck. They looked at each other helplessly.

"Edith Kalmar, will you allow Mr. Norbert Cameron to put his hand on your arm at certain times?"

Edith nodded.

"Say it aloud for the recording."

"Yes."

Norbert put his hand on her arm.

"Edith Kalmar," Professor Roberts said, "please tell us from the beginning what happened."

"It started with the tree, with Anna's tree. I was one of the last to go out, and then I saw that the tree was lying on the ground. The pot was broken. I wanted to pick up the tree and plant it again, but someone came...Miriam came and said no."

"You are lying," Miriam said. "Why don't you tell the truth, that you deliberately threw the tree down?"

Norbert took his hand away so everyone in the room could see it.

"Yes. No. Maybe I threw it down myself. I don't know."

"Please rest your hand on Edith Kalmar's arm again," Professor Roberts said. "So, Edith Kalmar, what's the truth?"

"Miriam said no and looked so strange. I was quite confused and didn't do anything with the tree. The next day, I wanted to talk to Anna, but Julius was so angry with the person who threw down the tree that I got scared."

"Why are you lying, Edith?" Miriam asked. "Why are you so hateful against me that you want to accuse me, even though I'm innocent?"

Norbert raised his hand again and Edith said, "I don't know. Yes, you are innocent."

She started to cry.

"I put my hand on Edith Kalmar's arm again. When I as a thought controller touch her arm, I erase the thought control exercised by another person on Edith Kalmar."

This statement swept like a storm through the assembly. Many of the people in the room leaned toward each other, whispering and murmuring, and some shook their heads.

The director asked, "Edith Kalmar, did you throw the tree down?"

"No."

"Did Miriam Andersson tell you to leave the tree on the ground?"

"Yes."

"Did she tell you to fly Benjamin Cameron to the McGregor family's house?"

"Yes."

"Why didn't you wait for the door of the McGregor family's house to open after you knocked?"

"I had to turn back immediately."

"Does that mean," Angus McGregor asked, "that this little girl here, Miriam Andersson, has forced

Edith Kalmar with some kind of thought control to do things she did not want to do?"

"It looks like it, doesn't it?" Norbert said.

"That's impossible. Such a small, delicate girl like Miriam Andersson is not capable of that at all."

"Thank you, Mr. McGregor," Miriam said, turning to look him in the eye. "You seem to be the only one here who is for justice. Please be so good as to unlock the door for me so that I can just fly home."

Angus McGregor, this bear of a man, stood up immediately.

"Oh, my goodness," Fiona said.

"Angus, no," Deirdre McGregor said.

He took a few quick steps toward the desk and reached for the key. But Norbert was faster. He took the key from the table and said to Miriam, "Stop immediately."

And to the others, he said, "When I put my hand on Edith Kalmar's arm, I wipe out Miriam Andersson's thought control on her. I can also temporarily interrupt Miriam Andersson's control of a person through my own ability of thought control without physically touching the affected person. However, this sudden cessation of thought control is a shock to the controlled person."

Angus McGregor stood in front of the desk as if someone had struck him on the head. He staggered, shook his head and asked, "What's going on?"

"Come sit down, Angus," Deirdre McGregor said.

And he sat down. "Suddenly I just wanted to do what Miriam Andersson told me. It seemed to be the reasonable thing to do. Is that thought control? But she is still so young. How can she do that?"

Angus McGregor looked at Miriam suspiciously from the side.

"Wendelin Roth," the director said, "would you please take the key here and unlock the door? Let in the people standing in front of the door and return the key to Mr. Norbert Cameron."

Anna took a deep breath when she saw who came in—Augusta with Benjamin in her arms.

Wendelin Roth led Augusta to the armchairs next to the Kalmar family and returned the key to Norbert.

"Mama, Dada," Benjamin said, smiling as he saw his parents.

"You can go to your parents in a moment, Benjamin Cameron," the director said, "but first I'd like to ask you a few questions. May I ask you?"

"Yes," the little boy said seriously.

"You were in the snow yesterday. Were you alone?"

"The girl flew away. I was alone."

"What did you do then?"

"I looked for a house. There was so much snow. It was cold."

"Did you find the house?"

"No, I fell in a hole. That was dark and cold."

"And what did you do then?"

Benjamin looked down.

"Well?" the director asked.

Benjamin said softly, "I'm not good. I'm bad."

"What did you do that was so bad? You can tell us without qualms. We all love you, no matter what you did."

"I called the sheep."

"And then?"

“The sheep came. I was warm.”

“You did well. If you are so cold, then you may call the sheep. Thank you, Benjamin Cameron. You helped us a lot. Now you can go to your parents.”

Anna had to smile when she saw the McGregors, Aquilases, and Kalmars thunderstruck again. Not her family. They already knew about Benjamin’s special gift.

Angus McGregor gasped. “Allow me to ask this question, Professor Roberts. Can this little boy make sheep come to him? Just like that—with his thoughts?”

“Yes, he can. The gift of thought control is present in only a few families. One of them is the Cameron family.

“Not all family members have this ability. It is strongly present in Norbert Cameron, and also in his little nephew Benjamin, who will study with the Council of the Wise in a few years, before studying at an academy at the age of ten.

“From what I have learned from Norbert Cameron, I assume that Anna Cameron inherited part of this ability. People with part of this gift notice when someone tries to control their thoughts and then unconsciously fight against it. Unfortunately, this defense consumes much of their life energy. Was that maybe what happened to you, Anna Cameron?"

"I think so," Anna said. "Is that why I got so tired and cold and confused when Miriam looked at me so intensely?"

The director nodded to her.

"Yes. As uncomfortable as that was, you had the advantage to realize that something was wrong. The real danger is that people without this gift do not even notice when they are being controlled."

"My goodness! Henry, it seems we have been thought-controlled by Miriam. I did not realize that. That's horrible." Tears ran down Maratha's face.

"Don't cry, Martha," Anna said, hugging her.

Henry cleared his throat.

"It's hard for me to grasp what I have just heard, but from what you have just said, Professor Roberts, I have to conclude that Martha and I were probably controlled by Miriam Andersson.

"Although the ability of thought control is inheritable in my family, there was never any abuse, as far as I know. We understood that a child of our family with this ability, as now our Benjamin, would train with the Council of the Wise at a certain age, and then everything would be fine.

“The fact that I did not realize that I had been controlled makes me feel deeply ashamed. Anna, please forgive me if I have wronged you during this time.” Henry swallowed.

“Oh, Henry, don’t be sad. That’s already forgiven. You’re the best father I could wish for.” She hugged her father.

Professor Robert said in a serious voice, “If the ability of thought control is used for selfish reasons, it is a great danger to us all.”

Angus McGregor was so agitated that his face turned nearly as red as his hair and beard. His blue eyes sparkled.

“You, Miriam Andersson, you seem to have that gift of thought control,” he said. “I believe that now. But there must be someone who has invented this complicated plan of abduction. You could never have planned this by yourself. Tell us—who has helped you?”

“What?” Miriam said. Her otherwise beautiful voice became shrill. “I could never have planned this by myself? You don’t give me credit for that? Do I have to have a big body with thick muscles like you to come up with a good plan? Of course, I planned it by myself."

Miriam looked around triumphantly, and everyone seemed to shrink back from her.

"For someone like me, it's easy," Miriam continued. "We students can fly to school with the school carpets and back home. All I had to do was fly to school with Benjamin and fly back to the Camerons so no one noticed I was gone.

"And Edith flew to school with her carpet and waited for me there. She then flew with Benjamin on the MacGregors' carpet to their house, then right back to school, and then home with her own carpet."

The director interrupted Miriam. "Edith Kalmar, did your parents not notice that you were gone for such a long time during the Winter Celebration?"

Now the otherwise pale Edith blushed. "We had so many relatives to visit, my parents didn't notice," she said, looking down at her folded hands. "When they saw me coming in, I told them I had been with the horses."

"Nevertheless, Miriam Andersson," said Angus McGregor, who was not to be stopped long, "I believe you now about the carpets. But how could you get Benjamin onto the carpet? You would have needed help after all. He certainly resisted?"

"That was ridiculously easy. After all, I have often watched Mrs. Cameron in her herbal kitchen. I knew where the narcotics were. All I had to do was lure the collie, which Benjamin particularly likes, behind the house and tie him up there.

"And then I waited for Benjamin to come outside again. He was always in and out. Then I kicked the dog, and he yelped. Benjamin came running, and I grabbed Benjamin from behind and held the rag with the anesthetic over his face.

"He quickly collapsed, and I could easily pull him onto the carpet. Then I untied the dog and flew to the academy. It was all very easy for me."

Miriam looked around triumphantly again, sat back in her chair, and stroked her long silver-blonde hair over her left shoulder.

An icy silence hung in the conference room. Martha, who held Benjamin on her lap, cried softly. Henry took her hand.

After a while, Lucius Aquilas cleared his throat. "I assume that someone has to be very close to Miriam

Andersson, like Angus McGregor, who is sitting next to her, for her to control their thoughts. It's not possible for her to control someone on the far side of the room like I am, right?"

"Oh, you really think so, Mr. Aquilas?" Miriam asked with a wicked smile as she looked at him intensely. "Don't you want to be so kind as to take the key and unlock the door to let me go?"

Serenely, Lucius Aquilas got up and walked calmly to the director's desk.

"Lucius, no," Sophia Aquilas called.

"The key, please," Lucius Aquilas said.

"Miriam, stop," Norbert said.

Lucius Aquilas staggered so much that he had to cling to the edge of the desk. He looked around helplessly.

"Sophia."

Sophia Aquilas came and led him to his chair. There he sat down and crossed his arms. Anna saw his hands trembling.

Julius stood up, shaking with indignation.

"I think you're smart enough to do it all, Miriam Andersson, but why? The Camerons are particularly fine and friendly people. Why?"

"Fine people! Especially Anna, yes?" She laughed scornfully.

"Anna, the beloved, who does not need me as a friend. Anna, who has Julius with the dragon as a friend. Anna, who immediately became friends with the carrot heads, the McGregors, but not with me.

"Anna, who does nothing special, but is nevertheless every teacher's favorite. She has everything. Her family is always there for her. Her little brother adores her, but she does not want anything to do with me. Like her little brother, who was against me from the start."

Miriam's words flowed out of her mouth like poison.

Professor Roberts said softly, "Friendship cannot be forced, Miriam Andersson."

The director got up. Norbert put his hand on her arm.

"Miriam Andersson," she said in a solemn voice, "with your deeds you have brought pain and heartache to a family that has shown you the friendliest hospitality. In addition, you have endangered the life of a little boy. Are you sorry for these acts?"

Miriam jumped up and looked at Anna with hatred. “No, no, and no again,” she cried. “Anna deserves all that and more!”

“Miriam Andersson,” Professor Roberts said, “I dismiss you from the Quentin Academy of Magical Arts and Sciences and hand you over to the Council of the Wise. Wendelin Roth, please take this key and open the door.”

In came two people in white robes. It seemed to Anna as if light streamed around them.

The woman was slim and tall with a rosy face under black hair. The man was even taller and looked very much like the director.

“I have the honor of introducing to you Electra White and Martin Roberts, my twin brother, both members of the Council of the Wise,” the director said.

The two people in the white robes bowed to the attendees.

Martin Roberts then said calmly, “Miriam Andersson, follow us.”

They turned and walked out, and Miriam followed them without a word.

Chapter 22

Lessons

Anna walked across the meadow with Julius to the Cameron's house. Kaylee and Amicus ran around them.

"Let's see how well we trained our dogs during the summer holidays," Julius said. "Amicus, sit."

Immediately, Amicus sat down.

"Kaylee, sit," she said, and Kaylee also sat down quickly.

"So far, so good," Julius said. "Let's see if they can wait obediently. Amicus, stay."

"Kaylee, stay," she said, moving on with Julius to her house.

She and Julius kept looking around as they walked on. The dogs sat where they were told, well-behaved, though obviously impatient.

"Amicus, come on."

"Kaylee, come on."

The dogs ran enthusiastically towards them.

"Now, give paw," she said.

"Oh no, not that silly paw giving again!"

"I think it's nice. Kaylee, sit. Give paw."

Kaylee handed Anna her right paw and looked very proud of it.

"Well done, Kaylee."

"Okay. Let's see if Amicus remembers the silly paw training. Amicus, sit. Give paw."

Amicus seemed to have nothing against paw giving.

Benjamin came to the meadow, followed by Hector and Toby, Norbert's collie.

"Oh, Norbert has arrived," she said. "Then it's tea time. By the way, Martha has baked your favorite cake, a plum cake."

"Are you doing give paw?" Benjamin asked when he came up. "I can do that, too. Hector, give paw."

Hector didn't even think about handing him his paw.

"Hector has a sense of honor," Julius said. "He's too proud to give his paw. He is right."

"But he has to do it if asked," she said. "Hector, sit. Give paw."

Hector sat down and reluctantly handed his paw to her.

Benjamin said, "Toby, sit. Give paw."

Toby sat down and looked expectantly at Benjamin, but he did not give his paw.

"Oh, no! Unfortunately, you can't tolerate him not giving his paw when he is asked to do so," she said. "Toby, give paw."

Toby wagged.

"He probably didn't learn such nonsense."

"We'll see. Toby, give paw."

Toby wagged again. He was a friendly dog.

"Yeah, it looks like Toby doesn't know what we want from him," she said.

Suddenly Toby turned around and handed Benjamin his paw.

"Bennie, no," she called.

Benjamin lowered his head.

When Anna woke up, she immediately remembered that tomorrow was the second of September, the day she would fly to the Quentin Academy of Magical Arts and Sciences for her second year at school.

She looked forward to seeing Fiona, Edith, and Duncan again. She also wanted to see Wendelin Roth, Professor Roberts, Professor Angelo, and unbelievably, the school itself.

"Good morning," the frog beside her pillow said. "Time to get up."

Now she was wide awake. Her frog? He sounded exactly like her frog. He looked the same as her frog. She touched him. He also felt like her frog. And his energy? Yes, it was him!

Kaylee got up and looked over the edge of the bed.

"Kaylee, my frog is back."

She stroked him and said, "Oh, give me another five minutes. It's just so cozy in bed."

The frog rolled his eyes.

About the Author

Brigitte Novalis is from Germany but now lives with her family near Boston, Massachusetts. She works as an intuitive healer, therapist, and Reiki Master.

Brigitte is also a motivational author and has written books, in both English and German, on rediscovering your joy of life, connecting with nature, and finding love.

As far back as she can remember, Brigitte has also loved fairy tales. Since her early childhood, she has marveled at tales of dragons, magic, and princes and princesses living in castles in faraway lands.

Brigitte is now devoting part of her time to writing fairy-tales, and also dreaming up new adventures at the Quentin Academy of Magical Arts and Sciences, which captivate children and adults alike.

You can connect with Brigitte online here:

`brigittenovalisbooks.com`

Thank you for reading this book. I hope you enjoyed it.

Feedback is an author's lifeblood. If you have a few moments to leave a review on Amazon or Goodreads, even if it's only a couple of lines, I'd be most grateful.

50225277R00141

Made in the USA
Middletown, DE
23 June 2019